This book belongs to

....

Magical Stories

Compiled by Vic Parker

Miles Kelly

First published in 2013 by Miles Kelly Publishing Ltd
Harding's Barn, Bardfield End Green, Thaxted, Essex, CM6 3PX, UK

This edition printed 2019

4 6 8 10 9 7 5

Publishing Director *Belinda Gallagher*
Creative Director *Jo Cowan*
Senior Editor *Carly Blake*
Designers *Jo Cowan, Joe Jones, Venita Kidwai*
Image Manager *Liberty Newton*
Production *Elizabeth Collins, Jennifer Brunwin-Jones*
Reprographics *Stephan Davis, Callum Ratcliffe-Bingham*
Assets *Lorraine King*

ISBN 978-1-78617-877-0

Printed in China

British Library Cataloguing-in-Publication Data
A catalogue record for this book is available from the British Library

ACKNOWLEDGEMENTS

The publishers would like to thank the following artists
who have contributed to this book:
Cover Morgan Huff at the Bright Agency
Other elements: Alice Brisland at The Bright Agency, LenLis/Shutterstock.com,
kusuriuri/Shutterstock.com, Lana L/Shutterstock.com and Markovka/Shutterstock.com
Inside pages
Advocate Art: Ghyslaine Vaysett (section templates), Alida Massari
The Bright Agency: Marsela Hajdinjak, Marcin Piwowarski, Tom Sperling

Made with paper from a sustainable forest

www.mileskelly.net

CONTENTS

ABOUT THE AUTHORS 8

ABOUT THE ARTISTS 12

CURIOUS CREATURES

The Crab that Played with the Sea 16

The Mermaid and the Boy 24

The King of the Polar Bears 35

The Unicorn 46

The Egg 58

Dapplegrim 65

The Frog 76

WISHES AND DREAMS

The Cinder-Maid · 86

A Grand Transformation Scene · · · · · · · · · · · · 98

The Stars in the Sky · 115

Beautiful as the Day · 122

The Three Wishes · 135

The Magical Mug · 139

An Unexpected Opening · · · · · · · · · · · · · · · · 147

The Lad Who Went to the North Wind · · · · · · · 153

MAGICAL PLACES

The Council with the Munchkins · · · · · · · · · · 162

The Mines · 175

The Buried Moon · 186

The Giant Builder · 196

Do You Believe in Fairies? · · · · · · · · · · · · · · · 209

Arndt's Night Underground · · · · · · · · · · · · · · 216

Shipwreck on Lilliput · · · · · · · · · · · · · · · · · · · 228

A Grin Without a Cat · · · · · · · · · · · · · · · · · · · 238

The Deliverers of their Country · · · · · · · · · · 244

ENCHANTMENTS AND TRANSFORMATIONS

The Enchanted Horse................................250

The Princess on the Glass Hill.............261

The Storks and the Night Owl.............274

The Feast of the Lanterns 288

The Old Man and the Gift 300

The Well of the World's End 307

The Crystal Coffin 313

MYSTERIOUS MORALS

The Baker's Daughter 322

Grasp All, Lose All 327

The Three Dwarves 337

The Paradise of Children.................347

The Hermit..............................358

Peter and the Magic Goose..............370

ABOUT THE AUTHORS

Find information below on some of the
authors whose stories appear in this book.

J M Barrie
1860–1937

James Matthew Barrie grew up in Scotland.
After graduating from the University of Edinburgh
in 1882 he became a journalist. Barrie eventually
moved to London where he became a novelist
and playwright, and is best known as the
creator of the Peter Pan character.

L Frank Baum
1856–1919

Lyman Frank Baum was born in New York, USA.
He hated his first name and preferred to be called
Frank. He began writing stories as a child, printing
them on his own printing press, and later worked as
a newspaper and magazine editor. Baum's greatest
success was *The Wonderful Wizard of Oz*. He went
on to write 13 books about the magical land of Oz,
and many other short stories, poems and scripts.

F Anstey
1856–1934

Thomas Anstey Guthrie used the pen name 'F Anstey'. He was a barrister in London before becoming a successful comic novelist. Many of his stories have been adapted for theatre and films.

Lewis Carroll
1832–1898

Lewis Carroll was the pen name of Charles Lutwidge Dodgson. He wrote poetry and short stories from a young age, but proved himself as a brilliant mathematician at Oxford University. He is most famous for his 'Alice' novels.

Sir George Webbe Dasent
1817–1896

After graduating from university, Dasent became a diplomat in Sweden. While there he met Jacob Grimm and became interested in folk tales. He went on to translate and publish several collections of ancient folk and fairy stories.

Joseph Jacobs
1854–1916

Born in Australia, Jacobs studied in England
and Germany as a young man, researching Jewish
history. Eventually he settled in America, and,
inspired by the Brothers Grimm, went on to
edit five collections of fairy tales.

Rudyard Kipling
1865–1936

Born to a British family in India, Kipling lived
in England from the age of five. He became one
of Britain's best-loved poets and children's
writers for works including *Just So Stories*
and *The Jungle Book*.

Andrew Lang
1844–1912

Scotsman Lang studied at St Andrew's
University in Fife and Balliol College, Oxford.
He researched folklore, mythology and religion,
and wrote poetry and novels. Lang adapted
12 books of folk and fairy tales for children.

E Nesbit
1858–1924

Edith Nesbit was born in Surrey, England. She began writing stories in her teens and went on to write and collaborate on over 60 children's books, several of which have been adapted for film and television. Her most famous novels include *The Railway Children* and *Five Children and It.*

Kate Douglas Wiggin 1856–1923
Nora Archibald Smith 1859–1934

Sisters Kate and Nora were born in Philadelphia, USA. Kate started the first free kindergarten in San Francisco. Then she and Nora set up a training school for kindergarten teachers, and raised money for it by writing stories. Together, they retold and edited many collections of tales for children.

ABOUT THE ARTISTS

Marsela Hajdinjak Marsela contributes to a number of children's magazines and has also created characters and scenography for several animated films. In 2005, she received the Grigor Vitez Award in recognition of her illustrations for the books _Water Sprite_ and _Old Pear Tree_. She lives and works in Zagreb, Croatia.

The Mermaid and the Boy • _The Stars in the Sky_ • _The Council with the Munchkins_ • _The Cinder-Maid_ • _A Grin Without a Cat_
The Storks and the Night Owl

Alida Massari Italian illustrator Alida has always been fond of art. She has travelled around Europe visiting old towns and galleries, both of which inspire her ancient-modern style. She has illustrated around 30 books, and works with acrylics, watercolours and collage.

The Crab that Played with the Sea • _The Unicorn_ • _Dapplegrim_
Do You Believe in Fairies? • _The Deliverers of Their Country_
The Well of the World's End

Tom Sperling After working at The Museum of Modern Art, New York, Tom pursued his interest in illustration by studying at The Art Student's League. He has twice been awarded the Paul Revere Award for Graphic Excellence and has won the Small Press Book Award for *The Wish Ring* for Best Illustrated Young Adult Book.

The King of the Polar Bears • A Grand Transformation Scene
Beautiful as the Day • The Mines • Shipwreck on Lilliput
The Princess on the Glass Hill • The Hermit • Grasp All, Lose All

Marcin Piwowarski From a very young age Marcin began painting, and he now specializes in children's illustration. His style is energetic, with multicultural references. Marcin's work has been published in the UK, Norway and the USA.

The Egg • The Frog • The Three Wishes • The Magical Mug
The Lad Who Went to the North Wind • The Buried Moon
Arndt's Night Underground • The Enchanted Horse • The Crystal
Coffin • The Baker's Daughter • Peter and the Magic Goose

The Crab that Played with the Sea   16

The Mermaid and the Boy   24

The King of the Polar Bears   35

CURIOUS CREATURES

The Egg 41

The Unicorn 46

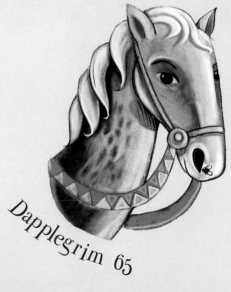

Dapplegrim 65

The Frog 76

The Crab that Played with the Sea

From the *Just So* stories
by Rudyard Kipling

Before the High and Far-Off Times, O my Best Beloved, came the Time of the Very Beginnings, and that was in the days when the Eldest Magician was getting Things ready. First he got the Earth ready, then he got the Sea ready, and then he told all the Animals that they could come out and play. And the Animals said, "O Eldest Magician, what shall we play at?"

And he said, "I will show you." He took the Elephant and said, "Play at being an Elephant," and the Elephant played. He took the Beaver and

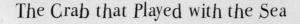

said, "Play at being a Beaver," and the Beaver played. He took the Cow and said, "Play at being a Cow," and the Cow played. He took the Turtle and said, "Play at being a Turtle," and the Turtle played. One by one he took all the beasts and birds and fishes and told them what to play at.

Towards evening, up came the Man, with his own best beloved little girl-daughter sitting upon his shoulder, and the Man said, "See that you make all the Animals obedient to me."

While the Man and the Eldest Magician were talking, Pau Amma the Crab, who was next in the game, scuttled off sideways and stepped into the sea, saying to himself, "I will play my play alone in the deep waters, and I will never be obedient to this son of Adam." Nobody saw him go except the little girl-daughter.

And the play went on till there were no more Animals left without orders, and the Eldest Magician wiped the fine dust off his hands and walked about the world to see how the Animals were playing.

He went North, East, West and South, and by and by the Eldest Magician met the Man on the banks of the Perak river, and said, "Ho! Son of Adam, are all the Animals obedient to you?"

"Yes," said the Man.

"Is all the Earth obedient to you?"

"Yes," said the Man.

"Is all the Sea obedient to you?"

"No," said the Man. "Once a day and once a night the Sea runs up the Perak river and drives the sweet-water back into the forest, so that my house is made wet. Once a day and once a night it runs down the river and draws all the water after it, so that there is nothing left but mud, and my canoe is upset. Is that the play you told it to play?"

"No," said the Eldest Magician. "That is a new

and a bad play. Launch your canoe and we will find out who is playing with the Sea."

They stepped into the canoe – the little girl-daughter came with them – and they pushed out on the Perak river and far out into the ocean. Then the Eldest Magician stood up and shouted, "Ho! Beasts, birds, and fishes, which one of you is playing with the Sea?"

Then all the beasts, birds, and fishes said together, "Eldest Magician, we play the plays that you taught us to play – we and our children's children. But not one of us plays with the Sea."

Then the little girl-daughter put up her little soft brown arms with the beautiful white shell bracelets and said, "O Eldest Magician! When my father here talked to you at the Very Beginning, one beast went away naughtily into the Sea before you had taught him his play. He was round and he was flat, and his eyes grew upon stalks, and he walked sideways like this, and he was covered with strong armour upon his back."

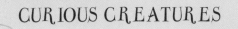

And the Eldest Magician said, "How wise are little children! Give me the paddle!"

So he took the paddle and paddled till they came to the place called Pusat Tasek – the Heart of the Sea. Then the Eldest Magician slid his arm up to the shoulder through the deep warm water, and touched the broad back of Pau Amma the Crab. Then the Eldest Magician called out, "What are you doing, Pau Amma?"

And Pau Amma, deep down below, answered, "Once a day and once a night I go out to look for my food. Once a day and once a night I return. Leave me alone."

Then the Eldest Magician said, "Listen, Pau Amma. When you go out from your cave the waters of the Sea pour down into Pusat Tasek.

When you come back and sit in Pusat Tasek, the waters of the Sea rise. If you are not afraid, come up and we will talk about it."

"I am not afraid," said Pau Amma, and he rose to the top of the sea, huge in the moonlight. No animal was as big as Pau Amma, for Pau Amma was King of all the crabs. "I didn't know I was so important," he said, rolling his eyes and waving his legs.

The Eldest Magician laughed. "You are not so important after all, Pau Amma," he said. And he made a Magic with just the little finger of his left hand – and lo and behold, Pau Amma's hard, rusty-copper-black shell fell off him as a husk falls off a coconut, and

Pau Amma was left all soft.

Then Pau Amma said, "What shall I do? I am so enormous that I can only hide in Pusat Tasek, and if I go anywhere else, all soft as I am now, the sharks and the dogfish will eat me. And if I go to Pusat Tasek, all soft as I am now, though I may be safe, I can never stir out to get my food, and so I shall die. "Then he waved his legs and lamented.

Then the Eldest Magician made a Magic with all five fingers of his right hand, and lo and behold, Best Beloved, Pau Amma grew smaller and smaller and smaller, till at last there was only a little coppery crab swimming in the water alongside the canoe.

And the girl-daughter took pity on him and gave him a pair of her scissors, and then Pau Amma was happier. He waved them in his little arms, and opened them and shut them and snapped them, and said, "I can eat nuts. I can crack shells. I can dig holes. I can climb trees. I can breathe in the dry air, and I can find a safe

Pusat Tasek under every stone. I did not know I was so important!"

And the Eldest Magician said, "I will give you back your shell, Pau Amma, for eleven months of the year, but on the twelfth month of every year it shall grow soft again, to remind you and all your children that I can make magics, and to keep you humble, Pau Amma."

And from that day to this, you can see when you go to the beach, how all Pau Amma's babies make little Pusat Taseks for themselves under every stone and bunch of weed on the sands, and you can see them waving their little scissors. But once a year all Pau Ammas have to shake off their hard armour and be soft – to remind them of what the Eldest Magician could do.

The Mermaid and the Boy

From Andrew Lang's
Brown Fairy Book

*L*ong ago, there lived a king who ruled over a country by the sea. Once, he had to leave his wife to visit his subjects in some distant islands. The king set off on the long sea voyage, but his ship soon ran upon a rock, and was stuck fast.

Suddenly a mermaid was seen dancing on the waves that threatened every moment to dash

24

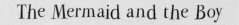

the ship to pieces. "There is only one way to free yourselves," she said to the king, "and that is to give me your solemn word that you will deliver to me the first child that is born to you."

Just then a huge wave broke with great force on the ship's side, and the king's crew fell on their knees and begged him to save them.

So he promised, and this time a wave lifted the vessel clean off the rocks, into the open sea.

In the fullness of time, a year after the king had returned home, he was overjoyed when the queen gave birth to a baby boy. But from that moment, he and the queen lived in terror, wondering if their son was to be snatched away.

When the prince was sixteen, the king and his wife decided that for his own sake, it would be best to send him into the world, for then perhaps the mermaid would never find him. The prince was delighted at the thought of adventures. He prepared a knapsack, bade farewell to his parents and set out.

All day he walked, till evening drew in. He was just about to stretch himself out on a soft mossy bank under a tree, when there was a fearful roar and a lion stood before him.

"Give me some food," said the lion, "it is past my supper time, and I am very hungry."

The boy was so thankful that the lion did not want to eat him, that he gladly picked up his knapsack and held out some bread and a flask of wine.

"I must be off now," remarked the lion, when he was done, "but if you are in any danger just wish yourself to be a lion and you will become one on the spot. One good turn deserves another, you know."

The prince thanked him for his kindness, and the two then bade each other farewell.

Next day, the boy again walked until evening drew in. Then he prepared a sleeping place in

some ferns. Suddenly there was a crashing noise and the boy saw a huge black bear thundering towards him.

"I am hungry," cried the bear. "Give me something to eat."

From his knapsack the prince took out his second flask of wine and another loaf of bread.

"I must go now," said the bear, when he was done, "but when you are in any danger just wish yourself to be a bear and you will become one. One good turn deserves another, you know."

And the boy and the bear bade each other farewell.

On the third day, the prince once again walked until evening drew in, whereupon he threw himself down under a tree to rest. Then, he heard a great buzzing over his head.

"I am hungry," said a bee in a cross voice. "Give me something to eat."

The boy took his last loaf and flask out of his knapsack and laid them on the ground, and they

had supper together.

"I must be off," said the bee when he was done. "But if you are in danger just wish yourself to be a bee and you will become one. One good turn deserves another, you know." And the bee departed.

Next day, the boy walked and walked until he entered a great city. He listened to the people gossiping and heard much talk about the king's only daughter, who was extremely beautiful.

The prince waited until everyone had gone to bed, then he wished himself to be a bee, and flew through the keyhole in the front door of the palace, up the great stairs, past the guards, and through the keyhole into the princess's chamber. Then he turned into a man again.

The princess, who was awake, was so startled that she couldn't even scream – she just sat up in bed gazing at him in silent terror.

"Do not be afraid," he said, "I shall not hurt you." And he began to praise her gardens, of which he had also heard the people speak, and the birds and flowers that she loved, till the princess's anger softened, and she answered him with gentle words. Indeed, she was so charmed by the prince that she vowed she would marry him, and confided to him that in three days her father would be off to the wars, leaving his sword in her room. If any man could find it and bring it to him he would receive her hand as a reward.

At this point the youth jumped up hastily saying, "Of course I shall ride with the king to the war, and if I do not return, take your violin every evening to the seashore and play on it."

Just as the princess had foretold, in three days the king set out for the war with a large following, and among them was the young prince. They had left the city many miles behind them, when the king suddenly discovered that he

had forgotten his sword, and though each and every one of his attendants immediately offered theirs, he declared that he could fight with none but his own.

"The first man who brings it to me from my daughter's room," cried he, "shall not only have her to be their wife, but after my death shall reign in my stead."

At this the young prince, a Red Knight, and several more turned their horses to ride as fast as the wind back to the palace. But suddenly a better plan entered the prince's head, and, letting the others pass him, he wished himself to be a lion. Then on he bounded, uttering such dreadful roars that the horses were frightened and grew unmanageable, and he easily outstripped them, and soon reached the gates of the palace. Here he hastily changed himself into a bee, and flew straight into the princess's room, where he became a man again. She showed him where the sword hung concealed behind a curtain, and he took it down, saying as he did so, "Be sure not to forget what you have promised to do."

The princess made no reply, but smiled sweetly, and slipping a golden ring from her finger she broke it in two and held half out to the prince, while the other half she put in her pocket. He kissed it, and ran down the stairs with the sword.

On his way back to the king, he stopped at a stream. Unbuckling the sword, he flung himself on the ground for a long drink. Unluckily, the mermaid happened at that moment to be floating on the water not very far off, and knew he was the boy who had been given to her before he was born. So she floated gently up, seized his arm, and the waves closed over them both. Hardly had they disappeared, when the Red Knight came by – he could scarcely believe his eyes when he saw the king's sword on the bank. He fastened it to his belt and carried it off to the king.

When the war was over and the king and his company returned, the princess saw to her great dismay that her true love was not among them. Moreover, the king told the poor princess that the Red Knight had won her fairly, and that the wedding would take place the very next day.

That evening, taking her violin under her arm, the princess crept down to the shore as she had promised the prince.

"Listen!" said the mermaid to the prince, who was lying stretched on a bed of seaweeds at the bottom of the sea. "Listen! That is your old love playing."

"I hear nothing," answered the youth, who did not look happy. "Take me up higher, where the sounds can reach me."

So the mermaid took him on her shoulders and bore him right up to the surface. "Can you hear now?" she asked.

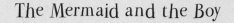

As soon as the prince thrust his head and
shoulders into the air, he wished himself to be a
bee, and flew straight into the pocket of the
princess. The mermaid looked in vain for him all
night, but he never came back, and never more
did he gladden her eyes.

But the princess felt that something strange
was about her, and returned quickly to the palace,
where the young man at once resumed his own
shape. Oh, what joy filled her heart at the sight of
him! But there was no time to be lost, and she led
him into the great hall, where the king and his
nobles were sitting feasting.

"Behold the gallant prince who fetched your
sword by the powers of his great magic!" the
princess announced. To prove it, the prince
turned himself into a lion, and the Red Knight
quaked with fear. Then the prince turned himself
into a bear, and the Red Knight hid behind the
princess. Then the prince turned himself into a
bee, and stung the Red Knight repeatedly until

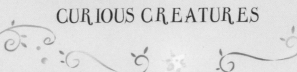

he fled the palace, never to be seen again.

How the king and his nobles laughed with joy! The princess drew out her half of the golden ring and showed how it fitted the prince's half . The next day, there was indeed a marriage feast for the princess and her true prince.

The King of the Polar Bears

From *American Fairy Tales*
by L Frank Baum

The King of the Polar Bears lived among the icebergs in the deep cold of the far north country. He was old, monstrous big, and very wise. His body was thickly covered with long, white hair that glistened silver under the midnight sun. His claws were strong and sharp, that he might walk over the smooth ice or grasp and tear the fishes and seals upon which he fed.

The seals were afraid of him, but the gulls – both white and grey – loved him because he left the remnants of his feasts for them.

Often his subjects, the polar bears, came to him for advice when they were ill or in trouble, but they kept away from his hunting grounds, lest they might arouse his anger.

The wolves, who sometimes came as far north as the icebergs, whispered among themselves that the King of the Polar Bears was a magician. For no earthly thing seemed able to harm him – he never failed to secure plenty of food, and he grew bigger and stronger day by day.

Yet the time came when this monarch of the north met man, and his wisdom failed him.

He came out of his cave among the icebergs one day and saw a boat moving through a strip of water uncovered by the shifting of the summer ice. In the boat were men.

The great bear had never seen such creatures before, and advanced sniffing the strange scent with aroused curiosity.

When the king came near the water's edge a man stood up in the boat and with a queer

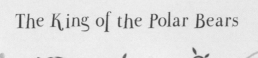

instrument made a loud 'Bang!' The polar bear felt a shock, his brain became numb, his thoughts deserted him, his great limbs shook and gave way beneath him and his body fell heavily upon the hard ice.

That was all he remembered for a time.

When he awoke he was smarting with pain on every inch of his huge bulk, for the men had cut away his hide with its glorious white hair and carried it with them to a distant ship.

Above him circled thousands of his friends, the gulls, wondering if their benefactor were really dead and it was proper to eat him. But when they saw him raise his head and groan and tremble they knew he still lived, and one of them said to his comrades, "The wolves were right. The

king is a great magician, for even men cannot kill him. But he suffers greatly for lack of covering. Let us repay his kindness to us by each giving him as many feathers as we can spare."

One after another they plucked with their beaks the softest feathers from under their wings, and, flying down, dropped them gently upon his body.

Then they called to him in a chorus, "Our feathers are as soft and beautiful as your own shaggy hair. They will guard you from the cold winds and warm you while you sleep."

And the King of the Polar Bears had courage to bear his pain and lived and was strong again.

The rest of that summer and all through the six months of night the king left his icy cavern only to fish or catch seals for food. He felt no shame at his feathery covering, but it was still strange to him, and he avoided meeting any of his brother bears.

When the moon fell away from the sky and the sun came to make the icebergs glitter with the

gorgeous tintings of the rainbow, two of the polar bears arrived at the king's cavern to ask his advice about the hunting season. But when they saw his great body covered with feathers instead of hair they began to laugh, and one said, "Our mighty king has become a bird! Who ever before heard of a feathered polar bear?"

Then the king gave way to wrath. He advanced upon them with deep growls and stately tread and with one blow of his monstrous paw stretched the mocker lifeless at his feet.

The other ran away to his fellows and carried the news of the king's strange appearance. The result was a meeting of all the polar bears upon a broad field of ice, where they talked gravely of the remarkable change that had come upon their monarch.

"He is, in reality, no longer a bear," said one, "nor can he justly be called a bird. But he is half bird and half bear, and so he is unfit to remain our king."

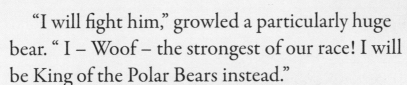

"I will fight him," growled a particularly huge bear. " I – Woof – the strongest of our race! I will be King of the Polar Bears instead."

The others nodded agreement, and dispatched a messenger to the king to say he must fight the great Woof and beat him, if he would stay ruler.

When the king heard this he visited his friends the gulls, and told them of the coming battle. "I shall conquer," he said, proudly. "Yet my people are right, for only a hairy one like themselves can hope to command their obedience."

The queen gull said, "I met an eagle yesterday, who had flown over a big city of men. The eagle told me he had seen a monstrous polar bear skin thrown over the back of a carriage that rolled along the street. That skin must have been yours, oh king, and if you wish I will send one hundred of my gulls to the city to bring it back to you."

"Let them go!" said the king, gruffly. And the hundred gulls were soon flying rapidly southward.

For three days they flew straight as an arrow,

until they came to scattered houses, to villages, and to cities. Then their search began.

The gulls were brave, cunning and wise. Upon the fourth day they reached the great metropolis, and hovered over the streets until a carriage rolled along with a great white bear robe thrown over the back seat. Then the birds swooped down and, seizing the skin in their beaks, flew quickly away.

They were late. The king's great battle was upon the seventh day, and they must fly swiftly to reach the Polar regions by that time.

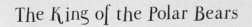

Meanwhile the bird-bear was preparing for his fight. He sharpened his claws in the small crevasses of the ice. He caught a seal and tested his big yellow teeth by crunching its bones between them. And the queen gull set her band to pluming the king bear's feathers until they lay smoothly upon his body.

But every day they cast anxious glances into the southern sky, watching for the hundred gulls to bring back the king's own skin.

The seventh day came, and all the polar bears in that region gathered around the king's cavern. Among them was Woof, confident of his success.

"The bird-bear's feathers will fly fast enough when I get my claws upon him!" he boasted, and the others laughed and encouraged him.

The king was sad at not having recovered his skin, but he resolved to fight bravely without it. He advanced from his cavern with a kingly bearing, and when he faced his enemy he gave so terrible a growl that Woof's heart stopped

beating for a moment, and he began to realize that a fight with the wise and mighty king of his race was no laughing matter.

After exchanging a few heavy blows with his foe Woof's courage returned, and he decided to dishearten his adversary by bluster.

"Come nearer, bird-bear!" he cried, "So that I may pluck your plumage!"

Filled with rage, the king ruffled his feathers till he seemed to be twice his actual size. He struck Woof a blow that cracked his skull like an egg-shell and he fell flat upon the ground.

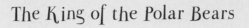

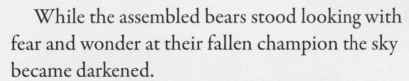

While the assembled bears stood looking with fear and wonder at their fallen champion the sky became darkened.

One hundred gulls flew down from above and dropped upon the king's body a skin covered with pure white hair that glittered in the sun like silver.

And behold! The bears saw before them the well-known form of their wise and respected master, and with one accord they bowed their shaggy heads in homage to the mighty King of the Polar Bears.

The Unicorn

From *Tales of Wonder Every Child Should Know*
by Kate Douglas Wiggin and
Nora Archibald Smith

Fritz, Franz and Hans were charcoal-burners who lived with their mother in the depths of a forest. Once upon a time they had been well off, but their father had died and all their money had been used up. Now their house was a poor hut and they scarcely had enough food for barely one meal a day. Fritz and Franz were, unfortunately, selfish, unpleasant lads, but Hans always had a cheerful smile or word, and did all in his power to help his mother to keep in good spirits.

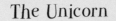

One day, at dinner time, they were startled by a knock at the door. Fritz growled out, in his usual surly tone, "Come in." The door opened, and a huntsman came in, who had been shooting game in the forest.

"Good morning, good friends," he said, in a cheerful tone. "Could you provide me with a cup of water and a mouthful of something to eat? I have forgotten to bring anything with me, and am ravenously hungry, and far from home."

Fritz and Franz threw a scowling glance from under their eyebrows and continued munching at their hunks of bread. Hans, however, was more polite. He invited the visitor to sit down, then filled a cup from a spring of delicious, cool water, which rose near the hut. He handed his own coarse crust to the stranger, saying he was sorry that there was nothing better to offer him.

"Thank you," said the stranger, courteously. He made short work of them, rolling the crumbs that fell from the crust into a hard pellet. Then he rose

to go. "Well, I thank you heartily for your hospitality," said the huntsman, "now I will give you a word of advice. One of you lads should go and seek the sparkling golden water, which turns everything it touches into gold."

Fritz and Franz pricked up their ears at this, and both at once demanded where this sparkling golden water was to be found. The stranger replied, "The sparkling golden water is to be found in the forest of dead trees, on the farther side of those blue mountains in the far distance." Then, bowing to his hosts, he stepped towards the door.

Hans, opened it for him and, obeying a sign from the stranger, followed him a little way from the hut. Then the stranger, taking from his pocket the little black bread pellet, said, "Keep this pellet carefully, and when you seek the sparkling golden water, as I know you will, don't forget to bring it with you." So saying, the stranger waved his hand to Hans, and, plunging into the thicket, disappeared.

Hans slipped the pellet into his pocket and
returned to the hut, where he found his brothers
in loud dispute about the sparkling golden water
– for each wanted to make a fortune for
themselves. At last it was decided, after a great
deal of squabbling, that Fritz as the eldest should
go in search first, and accordingly the next day he
set out. As he had no money he was forced to beg
at the doors of the cottages and farmhouses that
he passed, for food and shelter for the night.
Eventually he found himself approaching a vast
forest of enormous trees, which lifted leafless,
sapless branches to the sky, and every breath of
wind rattled them together like the bones of a
skeleton. Suddenly there was a terrible roaring
sound and out of the forest rushed a huge unicorn
with a spiral golden horn on his forehead.

"What seek you here?" asked the unicorn, in a
voice of thunder.

Fritz stammered out that he sought the

sparkling golden water.

The unicorn stamped furiously on the ground with his right forefoot. "Say this instant," he cried, "what it is that you want with the sparkling golden water!"

"I want to get money to buy land and become a count," Fritz was just able to gasp out.

The unicorn said nothing – he simply lowered his head, and with his golden horn tossed Fritz three hundred and forty-five feet in the air. Up went Fritz like a sky-rocket, and down he came, through the branches of one of the trees until he reached the point where

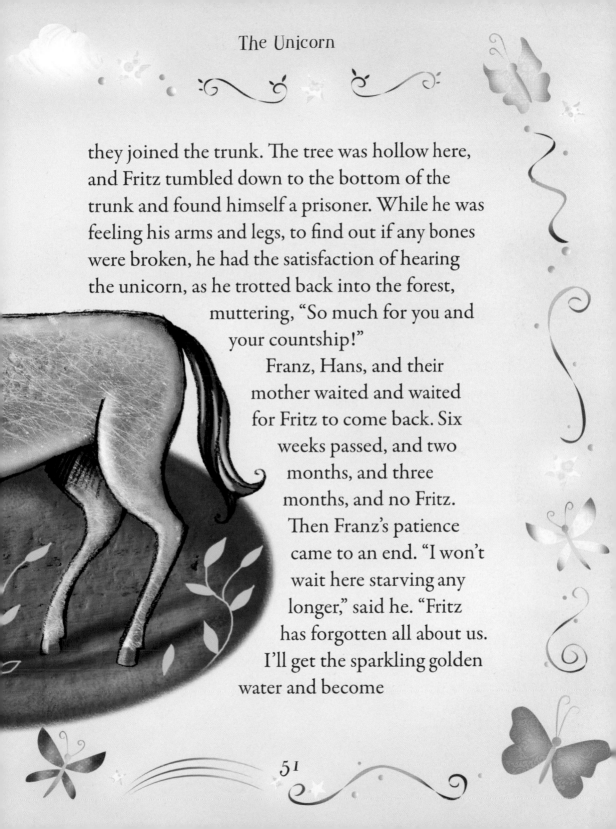

they joined the trunk. The tree was hollow here, and Fritz tumbled down to the bottom of the trunk and found himself a prisoner. While he was feeling his arms and legs, to find out if any bones were broken, he had the satisfaction of hearing the unicorn, as he trotted back into the forest, muttering, "So much for you and your countship!"

Franz, Hans, and their mother waited and waited for Fritz to come back. Six weeks passed, and two months, and three months, and no Fritz. Then Franz's patience came to an end. "I won't wait here starving any longer," said he. "Fritz has forgotten all about us. I'll get the sparkling golden water and become

Burgomaster." So off he set, following the same road as Fritz.

Eventually, Franz, very hungry and sulky, reached the verge of the forest of dead trees. Out came the unicorn and asked his business. On Franz replying that he wanted the sparkling golden water to buy the house and post of Burgomaster, the unicorn tossed him into the air, and he tumbled into the same tree as Fritz. Then the unicorn trotted back into the forest, muttering, for Franz's benefit, "So much for you and your Burgomastership!"

The months passed by, but no news came to Hans and his mother of Fritz and Franz. Eventually there was nothing for it but to leave his mother in the care of a kindly neighbour and go and see if he could find out what had become of them. By making enquiries Hans easily found the road that they had taken. At last he, too, found himself on the verge of the forest of dead trees and face to face with the golden-horned

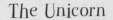

unicorn. But in reply to the usual question, given in the usual tone of thunder, Hans replied, coolly, "I seek my brothers, Fritz and Franz."

"They are where you will never find them," said the unicorn, "so go home again."

"If I cannot find my brothers," said Hans, firmly, "I will not go home without the sparkling golden water."

"What do you want with the sparkling golden water, which is in my charge?" asked the unicorn, in his terrible voice.

"I want to buy food and wine and comforts for my mother, who is very ill," answered Hans, undaunted. But his eyes filled with tears as he thought of his mother.

The unicorn spoke more gently.

"Do you have the crystal ball?" he asked. "Because without it I cannot allow you to pass to the sparkling golden water."

"The crystal ball!" echoed Hans. "I never heard of such a thing."

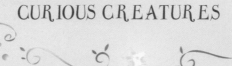

"That's a pity," said the unicorn, gravely. "I'm afraid you will have to go home without the water. But, stay, feel in your pockets. You may have had the ball, and put it somewhere, and have forgotten it."

"No," Hans said to the unicorn, "I have nothing in my pocket, except this pellet," and he was about to throw it away when the unicorn called out to him to stop.

"Why," the unicorn went on, "this is the crystal ball – look!"

Hans did look, and sure enough he found in his hand a tiny globe of crystal.

"Your possession of the crystal ball makes me your servant," declared the unicorn. "It is my duty

to carry you to the fountain of sparkling golden water, if you wish to go."

So Hans clambered onto the unicorn's back and grasped his mane. Then the unicorn gave a bound that carried him over the tops of the highest trees. Three such bounds did he take, and then he paused and said to Hans, "Now you may open your eyes." Hans found himself in a desolate, rocky valley, in the middle of which there sprang up a fountain of water, which sparked with such intense brilliancy that Hans was unable to look upon it at first.

"There, master," said the unicorn, turning his head, "this is the fountain of sparkling golden water. Dismount, and fill your flask. But take care that you do not allow your hand to touch the water. If it does it will be turned into gold, and will never become flesh and blood again."

Hans slipped quickly from his seat and, flask in hand, approached the fountain. He tried to be as careful as he possibly could be when filling the

flask, but, despite his greatest care, the top joint of his little finger briefly touched the golden water, and in an instant it became gold. However, he had his flask full of sparkling golden water, the flask itself was now, of course, golden, and he felt that the top joint of his little finger was really a small price to pay for all this.

"Where now, master?" said the unicorn when Hans got back.

"Take me to my brothers!" Hans asked. And the unicorn sprang away.

In the blink of an eye they were back in the dead forest. The unicorn led Hans to the tree in which his brothers were imprisoned, where they had been surviving on beetles, worms and rainwater. With one or two powerful blows with his horn, the unicorn made a hole large enough for the unhappy prisoners to creep out. Two more sheepish, miserable wretches than those half-starved brothers of his, Hans had never seen. They fell at his feet and thanked him again and

again for delivering them, and they promised never to do anything unkind or selfish again.

So did the brothers keep their promise? And did the sparkling golden water make Hans and his mother wealthy and happy? Well, that's another story...

The Egg

An extract from
The Phoenix and the Carpet
by E Nesbit

*Five children – Cyril, Anthea, Robert, Jane, and the youngest,
'the Lamb', are in their playroom. Their mother recently bought a
new carpet for the room. It was delivered rolled up, and when the
children laid it out, they found inside a strange golden egg,
which they have placed on the mantelpiece...*

"*I* wish they taught magic at school," Jane sighed.
"I believe if we could do a little magic it might
make something happen."

"I wonder how you begin?" Robert looked
round the room, but he got no ideas from the
faded green curtains, or the drab Venetian blinds,

or the worn brown oil-cloth on the floor. Even the new carpet suggested nothing, though its pattern was a very wonderful one, and always seemed as though it were just going to make you think of something.

"I could begin," said Anthea, "I've read about it. But I believe it's wrong in the Bible."

"It's only wrong in the Bible because people might use it to hurt other people. We don't want to hurt anybody, and what's more, we jolly well couldn't if we tried. Let's get the *Ingoldsby Legends*. There's a thing about Abra-cadabra there," said Cyril, yawning.

"I'll get *Ingoldsby,*" said Anthea. "You turn up the hearthrug."

So they traced strange figures on the linoleum, where the hearthrug had kept it clean. They traced them with chalk that Robert had nicked from the top of the mathematical master's desk at school. They chanted the gloomiest songs they could think of. And of course, nothing happened.

So then Anthea said, "I'm sure a magic fire ought to be made of sweet-smelling wood, and have magic gums and essences and things in it."

"I don't know any sweet-smelling wood, except cedar," said Robert, "but I've got some ends of cedar-wood lead pencil."

So they burned the ends of lead pencil. And still nothing happened.

"Let's burn some of the eucalyptus oil we have for our colds," said Anthea.

And they did. It certainly smelled very strong. And they burned lumps of camphor out of the big chest. It was very bright, and made lots of horrid black smoke, which looked very magical indeed. But still nothing happened. Then they got some clean tea-cloths from the dresser drawer in the kitchen, and waved them over the magic chalk-tracings, and sang 'The Hymn of the Moravian Nuns at Bethlehem', which is very impressive. And still nothing happened. So they waved more and more wildly, and then Robert's

tea-cloth accidentally caught the golden egg and whisked it off the mantelpiece, and it fell into the fender and rolled under the grate.

"Oh, crikey!" said more than one voice.

And everyone instantly fell down flat on their fronts to look under the grate, and there lay the egg, glowing in a nest of hot ashes.

"It's not smashed, anyhow," said Robert, and he put his hand under the grate and picked up the egg. But the egg was much hotter than anyone would have believed it could possibly get in such a short time, and Robert had to drop it with a cry of "Bother!" It fell on the top bar of the grate, and then bounced right into the glowing red-hot heart of the fire.

"The tongs!" cried Anthea. But, alas, no one could remember where they were. Everyone had forgotten that the tongs had last been used to fish up the doll's teapot from the bottom of the water-butt, where the Lamb had dropped it. So the nursery tongs were resting between the

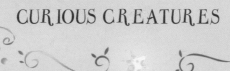

water-butt and the dustbin.

"Never mind," said Robert, "we'll get it out with the poker and the shovel."

"Oh, stop," cried Anthea. "Look at it! Quick, look! Look! Look! I do believe something IS going to happen!"

For the egg was now red-hot, and inside it something was moving. Next moment there was a soft cracking sound, the egg burst in two, and out of it came a flame-coloured bird. It rested a moment among the flames, and as it rested there the four children could see it growing bigger and bigger under their eyes.

Every mouth was a-gape, every eye a-goggle. The bird rose in its nest of fire, stretched its wings, and flew out into the room. It flew round and round, and where it passed the air was warm. Then it perched on the fender. Cyril put a hand towards the bird. It put its head on one side and

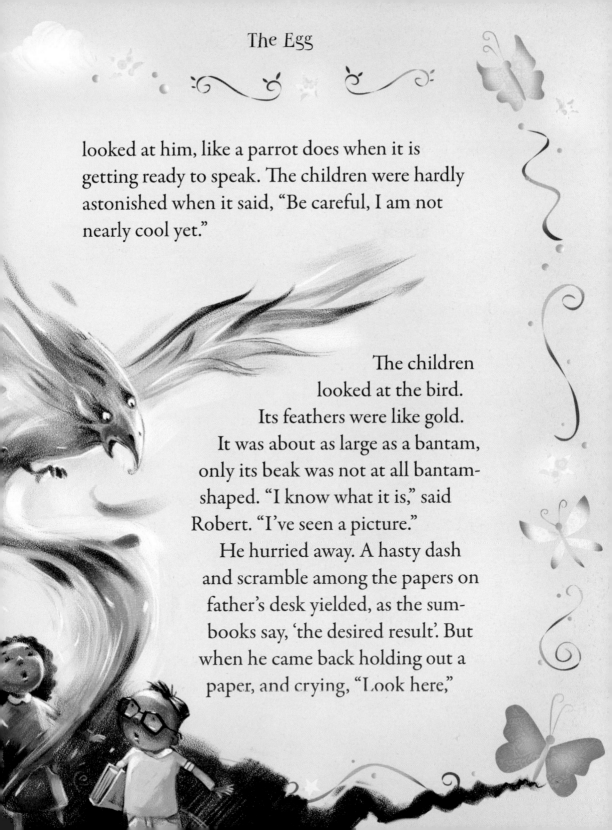

looked at him, like a parrot does when it is getting ready to speak. The children were hardly astonished when it said, "Be careful, I am not nearly cool yet."

The children looked at the bird. Its feathers were like gold. It was about as large as a bantam, only its beak was not at all bantam-shaped. "I know what it is," said Robert. "I've seen a picture."

He hurried away. A hasty dash and scramble among the papers on father's desk yielded, as the sum-books say, 'the desired result'. But when he came back holding out a paper, and crying, "Look here," the others all said, "Hush!" and he hushed obediently and instantly, for the bird was speaking.

"Who," it said, "put the egg into the fire?"

"He did," said three voices, and three fingers pointed at Robert.

The bird bowed – at least, it was more like that than anything else.

"I am your grateful debtor," it said with a high-bred air.

The children were all choking with wonder – except Robert. He held the paper in his hand, and said, "I know who you are." And he displayed the printed paper, at the head of which was a picture of a bird sitting in a nest of flames.

"You are the Phoenix," said Robert, and the bird was quite pleased.

Dapplegrim

From *Tales of Wonder Every Child Should Know*
by Kate Douglas Wiggin and
Nora Archibald Smith

Once on a time there was a rich couple who had twelve sons. When the youngest was grown up, he said he wouldn't stay any longer at home, but be off into the world to try his luck.

When he had walked a good bit, he came to a king's palace, where he asked for a place, and got it. Now, the king's daughter had been carried off into the hill by a troll. The king had no other children, so he and all his land were in great grief and sorrow, and the king gave his word that anyone who could set her free should have the

princess and half the kingdom. But there was no
one who could do it, though many tried.

When the lad had been there a year or so, he
longed to go home again, and back he went, but
his father and mother were dead, and his brothers
had shared everything between them. All that
was left were twelve old mares up on the hill.

However, the lad was content. He thanked his
brothers, and went to where the twelve mares
were at grass. One had a big dapple-grey foal, so
sleek that the sun shone from its coat.

"A fine fellow you are, little foal," said the lad.

"Yes," said the foal, "but wait another year to
pass, then see how big I'll be."

When the lad
came back the
following year, the
foal had indeed
grown. He was
such a big horse
that he had to lie

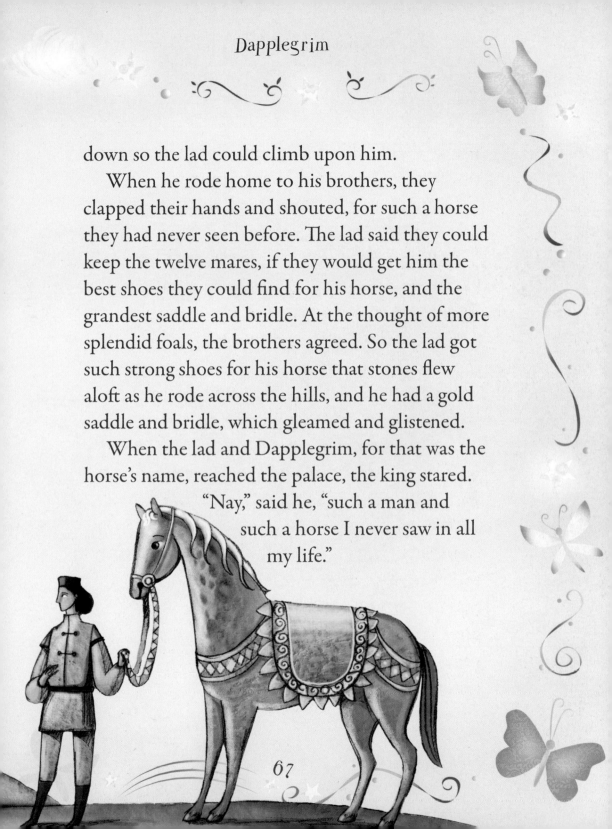

down so the lad could climb upon him.

When he rode home to his brothers, they clapped their hands and shouted, for such a horse they had never seen before. The lad said they could keep the twelve mares, if they would get him the best shoes they could find for his horse, and the grandest saddle and bridle. At the thought of more splendid foals, the brothers agreed. So the lad got such strong shoes for his horse that stones flew aloft as he rode across the hills, and he had a gold saddle and bridle, which gleamed and glistened.

When the lad and Dapplegrim, for that was the horse's name, reached the palace, the king stared. "Nay," said he, "such a man and such a horse I never saw in all my life."

The king was delighted to welcome the extraordinary lad and his steed back into his household. In fact, he gave him as much meadow-hay and oats as his horse could cram, and all the other knights had to lead their horses out of the stable that Dapplegrim might have it all to himself.

It wasn't long before all the others in the king's household began to be jealous of the lad, and there was no end to the bad things they would have done to him, if they had only dared. At last they thought of telling the king that he had been boasting he was man enough to set the king's daughter free – whom the troll had long since carried away into the hill – if he only chose. The king called the lad before him, and said he had heard what the lad had said, so now he must go and do it. If he succeeded, the king's daughter and half the kingdom should be his, and that promise would be faithfully kept. If he failed, he should be killed.

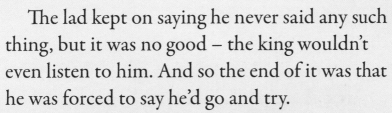

The lad kept on saying he never said any such thing, but it was no good – the king wouldn't even listen to him. And so the end of it was that he was forced to say he'd go and try.

So he went into the stable, down in the mouth and heavy-hearted, and told Dapplegrim why he was in such doleful dumps.

"This might be done, perhaps," said Dapplegrim. "But you must first have me well shod. You must go and ask for ten pounds of iron and twelve pounds of steel for the shoes, and one smith to hammer and another to hold."

Yes, the lad did that, and got for an answer, "Yes." He got both the iron and the steel, and the smith, and so Dapplegrim was shod very well, and off went the lad from the courtyard in a cloud of dust.

But when he came to the hill into which the princess had been carried, the difficulty was how to get up the steep wall of rock where the troll's cave was, in which the princess had been hidden.

For you must know that the hill stood straight up and down right on end, as upright as a house wall, and as smooth as a sheet of glass.

The first time the lad went at it he got a little way up, but then Dapplegrim's forelegs slipped, and down they went, with a sound that crashed like thunder on the hill.

The second time he rode at it he got some way further up, but then one foreleg slipped, and down they went with a sound like a landslip.

But the third time Dapple said, "Now we must show our mettle," and went at it again till the stones flew high about them, and so they got up.

Then the lad rode right into the cave at full speed, and caught up the princess, and threw her over his saddle-bow, and out and down again before the troll had time to even get on his legs.

"Thank you for freeing my princess," said the king to the lad, when he brought the princess into the hall and made his bow.

"She ought to be mine as well as yours, for

you're a word-fast man, I hope," said the lad.

"Ay, ay!" said the king. "But first we'll have one trial more, just to see whether you're fated to have her. First, she shall hide herself twice, and then you shall hide yourself twice. If you can find out her hiding-place, and she can't find out yours, why, then, you're fated to have her, and so you shall have her."

"That's not in the bargain, either," said the lad, "but we must try, since it must be so." And so the princess went off to hide herself first.

So she turned herself into a duck, and sat swimming on a pond that was close to the palace. But the lad ran down to the stable, and asked Dapplegrim what she had done with herself.

"Oh, you only need take your gun," said Dapplegrim, "and go down to the brink of the pond, and aim at the duck that lies swimming about there, and she'll soon show herself."

So the lad snatched his gun and ran off to the pond. "I'll just take a pop at this duck," he said, and began to aim at it.

"Nay, nay, dear friend, don't shoot. It is I," said the princess.

So he found her once.

And the second time the princess turned herself into a loaf of bread, and laid herself on the table amongst four other loaves, and so like was she to the other loaves, that no one could say which was which.

But the lad went again down to the stable to Dapplegrim, and said how the princess had hidden herself again, and he couldn't tell at all what had become of her.

"Oh, just take a good bread-knife," said Dapplegrim, "and do as if you were going to cut in two the third loaf on the left hand of those four loaves that are lying on the dresser in the king's kitchen, and you'll soon find her."

The lad was down in the kitchen in no time, and began to sharpen the biggest bread-knife he could lay his hands on. Then he caught hold of

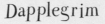
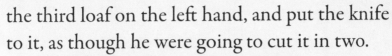

the third loaf on the left hand, and put the knife to it, as though he were going to cut it in two.

"I'll just have a slice off this loaf," he said.

"Nay, dear friend," said the princess, "don't cut. It is I."

So he found her twice.

Then he was to go and hide, but he and Dapplegrim had settled it so well beforehand that it wasn't easy to find him. First he turned himself into a fly, and hid himself in Dapplegrim's left nostril, and the princess went about hunting for him everywhere, high and low. At last she wanted to go into Dapplegrim's stall, but he began to bite and kick, so that she daren't go near him, and so she couldn't find the lad.

"Well," she said, "since I cannot find you, you must

show where you are yourself." In a trice the lad stood there on the stable floor.

The second time Dapplegrim told him just what to do. The lad turned himself into a clod of earth, and stuck himself between Dapplegrim's hoof and shoe on the near forefoot. So the princess hunted up and down, out and in, everywhere. At last she came into the stable, and wanted to go into Dapplegrim's loose box. This time he let her come up to him, and she pried high and low, but under his heels she couldn't, for he stood firm as a rock on his feet, and so she couldn't find the lad.

"Well, you must just show yourself, for I'm sure I can't find you," said the princess, and as she spoke the lad stood by her side on the stable floor.

"Now you are mine indeed," said the lad, "for now you can see I'm fated to have you." This he said both to the father and daughter.

"Yes, it does seem that it is so fated," said the king, "and so it must be."

Then everything was made ready for the wedding with great splendour and promptitude, and the lad and the princess got on Dapplegrim's back, and then, as you may guess, they were not long on their way to church.

The Frog

From Andrew Lang's *Violet Fairy Book*

Once upon a time there was a woman who had three sons. They were farmers, and the soil on which they lived was fruitful, and yielded rich crops. One day they all three told their mother they meant to get married. To which their mother replied, "Do as you like, but see that you choose good housewives – and, to make certain of this, take these three skeins of flax, and give it to them to spin. Whoever spins the best will be my favourite daughter-in-law."

Now the two eldest sons had already

chosen their wives, so they took the flax and carried it off with them, to have it spun as she had said. But the youngest son was puzzled what to do with his skein, as he knew no girl to whom he could give it to be spun. He wandered hither and thither, asking the girls that he met if they would undertake the task, but none would do so. Then he went out into the country and, seating himself on the bank of a pond, began to cry bitterly.

Suddenly there was a noise close beside him, and a frog jumped out of the water and asked him why he was crying. The youth told her of his trouble, and the frog said, "Do not weep. Give me the thread, and I will spin it for you." And, having said this, she took it out of his hand, and flopped back into the water, and the youth went back, not knowing what would happen next.

In a short time the two elder brothers came home, bringing with them the linen that had been spun by their chosen wives to show their mother. But the youngest brother was greatly troubled, for he had nothing to show. Sadly he took himself to the pond and, sitting down on the bank, began to weep.

Flop! And the frog appeared out of the water close beside him.

"Take this," she said, "here is the linen that I have spun for you."

You may imagine how delighted the youth was. He took the linen straight back to his mother, who declared she had never seen linen so beautifully spun. Indeed, she said it was far finer and whiter than the webs that the two elder brothers had brought home.

Then she turned to her sons and said, "But this is not enough, my sons, I must have another proof as to what sort of wives you have chosen. In the house there are three puppies. Each of you take one, and give it to the woman whom you mean to bring home as your wife. She must train it and

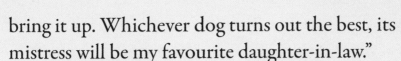

bring it up. Whichever dog turns out the best, its mistress will be my favourite daughter-in-law."

So the young men set out on their different ways, each taking a puppy with him. The youngest, not knowing where to go, returned to the pond, sat down once more on the bank, and began to weep.

Flop! And close beside him, he saw the frog. "Why are you weeping?" she said. Then he told her his difficulty, and that he did not know to whom he should take the puppy. "Give it to me," she said, "and I will bring it up for you." And she took the little creature out of his arms and disappeared with it into the pond.

The weeks and months passed, till one day the mother said she would like to see how the dogs had been trained by her future daughters-in-law. The two eldest sons departed, and returned shortly, leading with them two great mastiffs, who growled so fiercely, and looked so savage, that the mere sight of them made the mother

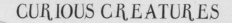

tremble with fear.

The youngest son went to the pond and called on the frog to come to his rescue.

In a minute she was at his side, bringing with her the most lovely little dog, which she put into his arms. It sat up and begged with its paws, and went through the prettiest tricks, and was almost human in the way it understood and did what it was told.

In high spirits the youth carried it off to his mother. As soon as she saw it, she exclaimed, "This is the most beautiful little dog I have ever seen. You are indeed fortunate, my son, you have won a pearl of a wife."

Then, turning to all three, she said, "Here are three shirts. Take them to your chosen wives. Whoever sews the best will be my favourite daughter-in-law."

So the young men set out once more, and again, this time, the work of the frog was much the best and the neatest.

This time the mother said, "Now that I am content with the tests I gave, I want you to go and fetch home your brides, and I will prepare the wedding-feast."

You may imagine what the youngest brother felt on hearing these words. Whence was he to fetch a bride? Would the frog be able to help him in this new difficulty? With bowed head, and feeling very sad, he sat down on the edge of the pond.

Flop! And once more the faithful frog was beside him. "What is troubling you?" she asked him, and then the youth told her everything. "Will you take me for a wife?" she asked.

"What should I do with you as a wife?" he replied, wondering at her strange proposal.

At this the frog disappeared. The next minute the youth beheld a lovely little chariot, drawn by two tiny ponies, standing on the road. The frog was holding the carriage door open for him to step in. "Come with me," she said. And he got up and followed her into the chariot.

As they drove along the road they met three witches. The first of them was blind, the second was hunchbacked, and the third had a large thorn in her throat. When the three witches beheld the chariot, with the frog seated among the cushions, they broke into such fits of laughter that the eyelids of the blind one burst open, and she recovered her sight, the hunchback rolled about on the ground in merriment till her back became

straight, and in a roar of laughter the thorn fell out of the throat of the third witch. Their first thought was to reward the frog, who had unconsciously been the means of curing them of their misfortunes.

The first witch waved her magic wand over the frog, and changed her into the loveliest girl that had ever been seen. The second witch waved the wand over the tiny chariot and ponies, and they were turned into a beautiful large carriage with prancing horses, and a coachman on the seat. The third witch gave the girl a magic purse, filled with money. Then the witches disappeared, and the youth with his bride drove to his mother's home.

The mother was delighted at her son's good fortune. A beautiful house was built for them, she was the favourite daughter-in-law, and they lived happily ever after.

The Cinder-Maid 86

A Grand Transformation Scene 98

The Stars in the Sky 115

Beautiful as the Day 122

WISHES AND DREAMS

The Three Wishes 135

The Magical Mug 139

An Unexpected Opening 147

The Lad Who Went to the North Wind 153

The Cinder-Maid

From *Europa's Fairy Book*
by Joseph Jacobs

Once upon a time, there was a king who had an only son, who was about to come of age. So the king sent round a herald to blow his trumpet and call out, "O yea, O yea, O yea, know ye that His Grace the king will give, on Monday week, a royal ball to which all maidens of noble birth are summoned, and be it furthermore known that at this ball His Highness the prince will select a lady to be his bride. God save the king."

Now there was among the nobles of the king's

court one who had married twice. By the first marriage he had one daughter. His wife died, and as the girl was growing up her father married again – a lady with two daughters.

His new wife, instead of caring for his first daughter, thought only of her own and favoured them in every way. She would give them beautiful dresses but none to her stepdaughter, who had only to wear the cast-off clothes of the other two. The noble's daughter was set to do all the drudgery of the house, and had nothing to sleep on but the heap of cinders raked out in the scullery, and that is why they called her Cinder-Maid. And no one took pity on her and she would go and weep at her mother's grave where she had planted a hazel tree, under which she sat.

You can imagine how excited everyone was when they heard the herald's proclamation.

"What shall we wear, Mother?" cried the two daughters, and they all began talking about dresses. But when the father suggested that

Cinder-Maid should also have a dress they all cried out, "What, Cinder-Maid going to the king's ball? Why, look at her, she would only disgrace us all." And so her father held his peace.

Now when the night came for the royal ball Cinder-Maid had to help the two sisters to dress in their fine dresses and saw them drive off in the carriage with her father and their mother. But she went to her own mother's grave and sat beneath the hazel tree and wept.

Then a little bird on the tree called out to her,

"Cinder-Maid, Cinder-Maid, shake the tree,
Open the first nut that you see."

So Cinder-Maid shook the tree and the first
nut that fell she took up and opened, and what
do you think she saw? A beautiful silk dress as
blue as the heavens, all embroidered with stars,
and two little lovely shoes made of shining
copper. And when she had dressed herself the
hazel tree opened and from it came a coach all
made of copper with four milk-white horses, with
coachman and footmen all complete. And as she
drove away the little bird called out to her,

"Be home, be home ere mid-o'night
Or else again you'll be a fright."

When Cinder-Maid entered the ballroom she
was the loveliest of all the ladies, and the prince,
who had been dancing with her stepsisters, would
dance only with her. But as it came towards
midnight Cinder-Maid remembered what the
little bird had told her and slipped away to her
carriage. And when the prince missed her he

went to the guards at the palace door and told them to follow the carriage. But Cinder-Maid when she saw this, called out,

"Mist behind and light before,
Guide me to my father's door."

And when the prince's soldiers tried to follow her there came such a mist that they couldn't see their hands before their faces. So they couldn't find which way Cinder-Maid went.

When her father and stepmother and two sisters came home after the ball they could talk of nothing but the lovely lady. "Ah, would not you have liked to have been there?" said the sisters to Cinder-Maid as she helped them to take off their fine dresses.

"There was a most lovely lady with a dress like the heavens and shoes of bright copper, and the prince would dance with none but her, and when midnight came she disappeared and the prince could not find her. He is going to give a second ball in the hope that she will come again.

Perhaps she will not, and then we will have our chance to dance with him."

When the time of the second royal ball came round the same thing happened as before. The sisters teased Cinder-Maid, saying, "Wouldn't you like to come with us?" and drove off again as before. And Cinder-Maid went again to the hazel tree over her mother's grave and cried.

And then the little bird on the tree called out,
"Cinder-Maid, Cinder-Maid, shake the tree,
Open the first nut that you see."

And this time she found a dress that was golden brown like the earth, embroidered with flowers, and her shoes were made of silver, and when the carriage came from the tree, lo and behold, that was made of silver too, drawn by black horses with trappings all of silver. And the lace on the coachman's and footmen's liveries was also made of silver.

When Cinder-Maid arrived at the ball the prince would dance with none but her, and when

midnight came round she fled as before. But the
prince, hoping to prevent her running away, had
ordered the soldiers at the foot of the staircase to
pour honey on the stairs so that her shoes would
stick in it. But Cinder-Maid leaped from stair to
stair and got away just in time, calling out as the
soldiers tried to follow her,

"Mist behind and light before,
Guide me to my father's door."

And when her sisters got home they told her
once more of the beautiful lady that had come in
a silver coach and silver shoes and in a dress all
embroidered with flowers. "Ah, wouldn't you
have liked to have been there?" said they.

Once again the prince decided to throw a
lavish ball in the hope that his unknown beauty
would come to it as she had before. And all *did*
happen as before – as soon as the sisters had gone
Cinder-Maid went to the hazel tree over her
mother's grave and wept. And then the little bird
appeared and said,

"Cinder-Maid, Cinder-Maid, shake the tree,
Open the first nut that you see."

And when she opened the nut, in it was a dress of silk as green as the sea with waves upon it, and her shoes this time were made of gold, and when the coach came out of the tree it was also made of gold, with gold trappings for the horses and for the retainers. And as she drove off the little bird from the tree called out,

"Be home, be home ere mid-o'night
Or else again you'll be a fright."

This time when Cinder-Maid came to the ball, she was as keen to dance with the prince as he was with her. They danced together all evening. So, when midnight came round, Cinder-Maid had forgotten to leave until the clock began to strike, one – two – three – four – five – six, and then she began to run as fast as she could down the stairs as the clock struck, eight – nine – ten.

However this time the prince had instructed his soldiers to place tar upon the lower steps of the stairs, and just as the clock struck eleven Cinder-Maid's shoes became stuck in the tar, and when she jumped to the foot of the stairs one of her golden shoes was left behind. Then the clock struck TWELVE, and the golden coach, with its horses and footmen, disappeared, and the beautiful dress of Cinder-Maid changed again into her ragged clothes and she had to run home with only one golden shoe.

You can imagine how excited the sisters were when they came home and told Cinder-Maid all about it, how the beautiful lady had come in a golden coach in a dress like the sea, with golden shoes, and how all had disappeared at midnight except the golden shoe. "Ah, wouldn't you have liked to have been there?" said they.

Now when the prince found out that he could not keep his lady-love nor trace where she had gone he spoke to his father and showed him the golden shoe, and told him that he would never marry anyone but the maiden who could wear

that shoe. So the king, his father, ordered the herald to take round the golden shoe upon a velvet cushion and sound the trumpet and call out, "O yea, O yea, O yea, be it known unto you all that whatsoever lady of noble birth can fit this shoe upon her foot shall become the bride of His Highness the prince and our future queen. God save the king."

And when the herald came to the house of Cinder-Maid's father, the eldest of her two step-sisters tried on the golden shoe. But it was much too small for her, as it was for every other lady that had tried it up to that time. And the herald asked, "Have you no other daughter?"

And the sisters cried out, "No, sir."

But the father said, "Yes, I have another daughter."

And the sisters cried out, "Cinder-Maid! She could not wear that shoe."

But the herald said, "As she is of noble birth she has a right to try the shoe." So the herald went down to the kitchen and found Cinder-Maid, and when she saw her golden shoe she took it from him and put it on her foot, which it fitted exactly. Then she took the other golden shoe from underneath the cinders where she had hidden it and put that on too. Then the herald knew that she was the true bride of his master, and he sent for the prince at once.

When the prince saw Cinder-Maid's face, he knew at once that she was the lady of his love. So he took her behind him upon his horse, and as they rode to the palace, the little bird from the hazel tree cried out,

"Some squashed their heel, and some squished their toe,
But she sat by the fire who could wear the shoe."

And so they were married and lived happy ever afterwards.

A Grand Transformation Scene

An extract from *Vice Versa* by F Anstey

Dick Bultitude is a Victorian schoolboy. The school holidays are at an end, and his father, Paul, is saying goodbye as Dick is about to set off back to boarding school, where he is very unhappy.

Mr Bultitude selected from the coins before him a florin, two shillings, and two sixpences, which he pushed across to his son, who looked at them with disappointment.

"That's a lot of pocket money for a young fellow like you," Mr Bultitude observed. "Don't buy anything foolish with it, and if, towards the end of the term you want a little more, and write an intelligible letter asking for it, and I think proper to let you have it – why, you'll get it, you know."

Dick had not the courage to ask for more, much as he longed to do so, so he put the money in his purse. There, he seemed to find something that had escaped his memory, for he took out a small parcel and unfolded it.

"I nearly forgot," he said, "I didn't like to take it without asking you, but may I have it?"

"Eh?" said Mr Bultitude, sharply. "What's that? Something else – what is it you want now?"

"It's only that stone Uncle Marmaduke brought Mamma from India – the thing, he said, they called a 'Pagoda stone', or something, out there."

"Pagoda stone? The boy means Garudâ Stone. I should like to know how you got hold of that – you've been meddling in my drawers, now, haven't you? A thing I will not put up with, as I've told you over and over again."

"No, I haven't," said Dick, "I found it in a tray in the drawing-room – but I may have it, mayn't I?" he persisted.

"Have it? You may certainly not. What could you possibly want with a ridiculous thing like that? Give it to me."

Dick handed it over reluctantly. It was not much to look at, a little square tablet of greyish green stone, pierced at one angle, and having on two of its faces faint traces of mysterious letters or symbols, which time had made very difficult to distinguish.

It looked harmless enough as Mr Bultitude took it – there was no kindly hand to hold him back, no warning voice to hint that there might possibly be sleeping within that small marble block the pent-up energy of long-forgotten Eastern magic, ready to awake into action at the first words that had power to stir it.

Paul Bultitude put on his glasses to examine the stone more carefully, for it was some time since he had last seen or thought about it. Then he looked up and said once more, "What use would a thing like this be to you?"

Dick would have considered it a very valuable prize indeed. He could have shown it to admiring friends under the desk during boring lessons, he could have played with it and invented astonishing legends of its powers, and when he had grown tired of it at last, he could have swapped it for something else. But he could not find either courage or words to explain himself. So he only said awkwardly, "Oh, I don't know, I would just like it."

"Well, anyway," said Paul, "you certainly won't have it. It must be worth something, whatever it is, as the only thing your Uncle Marmaduke was ever known to give to anybody."

"Isn't it a talisman, a charm, though?" said Dick.

"I'm sure I can't tell you," yawned Paul, "how do you mean?"

"I don't know, only Uncle Marmaduke once said something about it. Maybe it cures people of things – though I tried it once on my chilblains, and it wasn't a bit of good. If you would only let me have it, perhaps I might find out, you know."

"You might," said his father drily, "but you won't have the chance. If it has a secret, I will find it out for myself...and, by the way, I hear your taxi arriving – at last."

There was a sound of wheels outside, and, as Dick heard them, he grew desperate to ask for something else, something even more important. He got up and moved timidly towards his father.

"Father," he said, "there's something I want to say. Do let me ask you now."

"Well, what is it?" said Paul. "Make haste,

you haven't much time."

"It's this. I want you to... to let me leave Grimstone's at the end of the term."

"Let you leave Grimstone's!" said Paul angrily. "What do you mean? It's an excellent school!"

"I'd like to go to Marlborough, or Harrow, or somewhere else," whimpered Dick. "My friend Jolland's going to Harrow at Easter. The headmaster, Dr Grimstone, is nice enough to pupils he likes, but he doesn't like me – he's always blaming me for something – and I hate some of the other boys there, and altogether it's awful. Do let me leave!"

"It's all ridiculous nonsense, I tell you," said Paul angrily. "You will stay at Grimstone's for as long as I say, and there's an end of that!"

At this, Dick began to sob, which was more than his father could bear. To do Paul justice, he had not meant to be quite so harsh, and, a little ashamed, he sought to justify himself by running through all the reasons why Grimstone's was such a good school.

"Now, you know, it's no use to cry like that," he began. "It's the usual thing for boys at school, I'm quite aware, to go about fancying they're very hard done by, and miserable, and all the rest of it! It's one of those things all boys have to go through. And you mark my words, my boy, when they grow up and go out into the world, they look back at school as being the happiest time of their life!"

"Well," said Dick, "then I hope it won't be the happiest time in mine! You may have been happy at the school you went to, perhaps, but I don't believe you would very much care about being a boy again like me, and going back to Grimstone's!"

Paul still had the stone in his hand as he replied, smirking, "Perhaps you will believe me, when I tell you that, old as I am, I only wish that I could be a boy again, going back to school, like you."

As he spoke, he felt a shiver, followed by a curious shrinking sensation all over. And the armchair in which he sat seemed to have grown so much bigger all at once. He felt a passing surprise, but decided it must be his imagination, and went on as before.

"I should like it, my boy, but what's the good of wishing? I'm an old man and you're a young boy, and there's nothing anyone can... What the devil are you giggling about?"

For Dick, after some seconds of half-frightened and open-mouthed staring, had suddenly burst into a violent fit of sniggering, which he was trying hard to stop.

This naturally annoyed Mr Bultitude, and he went on with immense dignity, "I'm not aware that I've been saying anything particularly ridiculous. You seem to be amused?"

"Don't!" gasped Dick. "It, it isn't anything you're saying... it's, it's...oh, can't you feel any difference?"

"The sooner you go back to school the better!" said Paul angrily. "I've had quite enough of this. Leave the room this instant!"

Dick, however, remained where he was, choking and shaking with laughter, while his father sat stiffly on his chair, and tried to ignore his son's strange behaviour.

At last his patience gave out, and he said coldly, "Now, perhaps, you will be good enough to let me know what the joke is?"

Dick's voice was hoarse with laughter as he spoke. "Haven't you found out yet? Go and look at yourself in the mirror!"

Mr Bultitude walked to the mirror, wondering whether he had a smudge on his face or something wrong with his collar and tie. But no sooner had Paul met his reflection than he started back in horror – then returned and stared again, and again.

Surely, surely, this could not be he!

He had expected to see his own familiar, portly presence there – but somehow, look as he would, the mirror insisted upon reflecting the figure of his son Dick! Besides, the reflection opposite him moved when he moved, returned when he returned, copied his every gesture!

He turned round upon his son in anger. "You've been playing some of your tricks with this mirror," he cried fiercely. "What have you done to it?"

"Done! How could I do anything to it?"

"Then," stammered Paul, " do you mean to tell me you can see any – changes to my appearance? Tell me the truth now!"

"I should think so!" said Dick. "It's very queer, but just look here," and he came over to the mirror and placed himself by the side of his horrified father. "Why," he said, with another giggle, "we're as like as two peas!"

They were indeed. The glass reflected now two small boys, each with chubby cheeks and golden hair, both dressed, too, exactly alike, in Eton jackets and broad white collars. The only difference to be seen between them was that, while one face wore an expression of intense glee and satisfaction, the other – the one which Mr Bultitude was beginning to fear must belong to him – was lengthened and drawn with dismay and bewilderment.

"Dick," said Paul faintly, "what is all this? What has happened?"

"I'm sure I don't know, I haven't done anything!" protested Dick. "You can't be me, because here I am, you know. And you're not yourself, that's very plain."

"Never mind who I am," said Paul angrily. "I feel just the same as I always did. Tell me when you first began to notice any change."

"It was just as you were talking about going to school and all that. You said you only wished...Why of course – it must be the stone that did it!"

"Stone! What stone?" said Paul. "I don't know what you're talking about."

"Yes, you do – the Garudâ Stone! You've got it in your hand still. Don't you see? It is a real talisman after all! How amazing!"

"How perfectly absurd!"

"Well, something has definitely happened to you, hasn't it? And it must have been done somehow," argued Dick.

"I was holding the confounded thing, certainly," said Paul, "here it is. But what could I have said to start it? What has it

109

done this to me for?"

"I know!" cried Dick. "Don't you remember? You said you wished you were a boy again, like me. So you are, you see, exactly like me!"

"Wished!" echoed Mr Bultitude. "Why, of course – I never thought of that. The thing's a wishing stone – it must be! You have to hold it, I suppose, and then say what you wish aloud, and there you are. If that's the case, I can soon put it all right by simply wishing myself back again."

He took the stone, and got into a corner by himself where he began repeating the words, "I wish I was back again," and "I wish I was the man I was five minutes ago," and "I wish all this had not happened," and so on, until he was very exhausted and red in the face. He tried with the stone held in his left hand, as well as his right, sitting and standing, under all the various conditions he could think of, but absolutely nothing came of it – he was just as exasperatingly boyish and youthful as ever at the end of it.

"I don't like this," he said at last, giving it up with a rather crestfallen air. "It seems to me that this diabolical invention has got out of order somehow – I can't make it work any more!"

"Perhaps," suggested Dick, who still looked gleeful, "it's one of those talismans that only give you one wish, and you've had it, you know?"

"Then it's all over!" groaned Paul. "What the devil am I to do? Suppose your sister or one of the servants comes in and sees me like this! If I don't see my way out of this soon, I shall go raving mad!" And he paced restlessly up and down the room with his brain on fire.

All at once, an idea came to him. He was forced to agree that, improbable and fantastic though it might appear, there must be some magic power in this Garudâ Stone. It was plain too that the talisman would no longer work for him. But perhaps it would grant a wish for someone else? If Dick took the stone and wished that his father would return to normal, maybe everything would be put right.

Mr Bultitude explained his plan to Dick.

"I can try," Dick said, with a mischievous sparkle in his eye, "give the stone to me."

"Take it," said Paul, desperately. "Take it, and wish your poor old father himself again!"

Dick took the stone, and held it thoughtfully in his hand for some moments.

"I suppose," he asked, "when you are yourself again, things would go on just as usual?"

"I... I hope so."

"I mean you will go on sitting here, and I shall go off to Grimstone's?"

"Of course, of course," said Paul, "don't ask so many questions. I'm sure you quite understand what has to be done, so get on. We might be found like this any minute."

"That settles it," said Dick.

"Settles what?" asked Mr Bultitude, struck by something peculiar in the boy's manner.

"Well, I've thought of something fairer. You

see, you wished to be a boy just like me. Well, if I wish to be a man just like you were ten minutes ago, before you took the stone, that will put things all right again, won't it?"

"Are you mad?" cried Paul, horrified at this proposal. "Why that would be worse than ever! Give me back that stone. I can't trust you with it."

But Dick was too quick for him. Slipping off the table, he planted himself firmly on the hearthrug, with the hand that held the stone clenched behind his back, and the other raised in self-defence.

"I wish I was a man like you were just now!" he cried in triumph.

And as he spoke, Mr Bultitude had the bitterness of seeing his son swell into the exact copy of his former self!

The transformed Dick began to skip and dance round the room in glee. "It's all right, you see," he said. "The old stone's as good as ever. You can't say anyone would ever know, to look at us."

And then he threw himself panting into a chair, and began to laugh excitedly at the success of his brilliant idea.

The Stars in the Sky

From *More English Fairy Tales*
by Joseph Jacobs

*O*nce upon a time, there was a lassie who wept all day to have the stars in the sky to play with. She wouldn't have this, and she wouldn't have that, but it was always the stars she would have. So one day, off she went to find them. And she walked and walked, till by and by she came to a mill-dam.

"Goode'en to ye," says she, "I'm seeking the stars in the sky to play with. Have you seen any?"

"Oh, yes," said the mill-dam. "They shine in my face o' nights till I can't sleep for them. Jump in and perhaps you'll find one."

In she jumped and swam about, but ne'er a one could she see. She went on till she came to a brooklet.

"Goode'en to ye, Brooklet," says she. "I'm seeking the stars in the sky to play with. Have you seen any?"

"Yes, indeed," said the Brooklet. "They glint on my banks at night. Paddle about and maybe you'll find one."

So she paddled and paddled, but ne'er a one did she find. So on she went till she came to the Good Folk.

"Goode'en to ye, Good Folk," says she. "I'm looking for the stars in the sky to play with. Have ye seen e'er a one?"

"Why, yes," said the Good Folk. "They shine on the grass here o' night. Dance with us and maybe you'll find one."

And she danced and danced, but ne'er a one did she see. So down she sat and wept.

"Oh dearie me," says she, "I've swam and I've paddled and I've danced, and if ye'll not help me I shall never find the stars in the sky to play with."

But the Good Folk whispered together, and one of them took her by the hand and said, "Go forward – and mind you take the right road. Ask Four Feet to carry you to No Feet at all, and tell No Feet at all to carry you to the stairs without steps, and if you can climb that..."

"Oh, shall I be among the stars in the sky then?" cried the lassie.

"If you'll not be, then you'll be elsewhere," said the Good Folk, and set to dancing again.

So on she went again with a light heart, and by and by she came to a saddled horse, tied to a tree.

"Goode'en to ye, Beast," said she. "I'm seeking the stars in the sky to play with. Will you give me a lift, for all my bones are an-aching."

"Nay," said the horse, "I know naught of the stars in the sky, and I'm here to do the bidding of the Good Folk, not my own will."

"Well," said she, "it's from the Good Folk I come, and they bade me tell Four Feet to carry me to No Feet at all."

"Jump up and ride with me," said the horse.

So they rode and rode and rode, until they got out of the forest and found themselves at the very edge of the sea. And on the water was a wide glistening path running straight out towards a beautiful thing that rose out of the water and went up into the sky, and was all the colours in the world, blue and red and green, and very wonderful to look at.

The horse said, "I've brought ye to the end of the land, and that's as much as Four Feet can do."

"But," said the lassie, "where's No Feet at all, and where's the stair without steps?"

"I know not," said the horse. "Goode'en to ye." And off he went.

The lassie stood and looked at the water, till a strange kind of fish came swimming up to her feet.

"Goode'en to ye, big fish," says she. "I'm

looking for the stars in the sky, and for the stairs that climb up to them. Do you think you could show me the way?"

"Nay," said the fish, "I can't unless you bring me word from the Good Folk."

"Yes, indeed," said the girl. "They told me Four Feet would bring me to No Feet at all, and No Feet at all would carry me all the way to the stairs without steps."

"Ah, well," said the fish, "that's all right then. Get on my back and hold fast."

And off he went – *kerplash!* – into the beautiful water, along the silver path, towards the bright arch. And the nearer they came to it, the brighter the sheen of it, until the girl had to shade her eyes.

And as they came to the foot of it, she saw that it was a broad bright road, sloping up, up and away into the sky, and at the far, far end of it she could just about see the wee shining things dancing about.

"Now," said the fish, "here you are, and yon's the stair. Climb up, if you can, but hold on fast." And off he splashed through the water.

So she climbed and climbed, but ne'er a step higher did she get. The light was before her and around her, and the water behind her, and the more she struggled the more she was forced down into the dark and the cold, and the more she climbed, the deeper she fell.

But she climbed and climbed, till she got dizzy in the light and shivered with the cold, and dazed with the fear – and she let clean go, and sank down... down... down...

And – *bang!* – she landed on hard boards, and found herself sitting, weeping and wailing, by the bedside at home all alone.

Beautiful as the Day

An extract from *Five Children and It*
by E Nesbit

*Five children – Cyril, Anthea, Robert, Jane, and the youngest,
a baby whom they call 'the Lamb' – have moved house
from London to the countryside of Kent.*

The children had explored the gardens and the outhouses thoroughly before tea, and they saw quite well that they were certain to be happy at the White House. It was on the edge of a hill, with a wood behind it and the chalk-quarry on one side and the gravel-pit on the other. And it was at the gravel-pit that IT happened...

One day, the children decided to take their buckets and spades to dig in the pit, pretending they were at the seaside. They built a big castle, of course. Then Cyril wanted to dig out a cave to play smugglers in, but the others thought it might bury them alive, so it ended in all spades going to work to dig a hole through the castle to Australia. The children dug and they dug and they dug, and their hands got sandy and hot and red, and their faces got damp and shiny. The hole soon grew so deep that Jane begged the others to stop.

"Suppose the bottom gave way suddenly," she said, "and you tumbled out among the Australians, all the sand would get in their eyes."

"Yes," said Robert, "and they would probably hate us, and not let us see the kangaroos, or opossums, or eucalyptus trees, or emus, or anything."

Cyril and Anthea knew that Australia was not quite so near as all that, but they agreed to stop using the spades and go on with their hands. This was quite easy, because the sand at the bottom of the hole was soft and fine and dry, like sea-sand. And there were little shells in it.

Nevertheless, Cyril had soon had quite enough. "It's beastly hot in this Australian hole," he puffed. "Let's go and look for bigger shells – I think that little cave looks likely, and I see something sticking out there like a bit of wrecked ship's anchor."

The others agreed, but Anthea carried on digging the hole, because she liked to finish a thing once she had begun it.

The cave was disappointing – there were no shells, and the wrecked ship's anchor turned out to be only the broken end of a pickaxe handle, and the cave party were just making up their minds that the sand makes you thirstier when it is not by the seaside, and someone had suggested going home for some lemonade, when Anthea suddenly gave a loud scream.

"Cyril! Come here! Oh, come quick! It's alive! It'll get away! Quick!" They all hurried back to her.

"It's a rat, I shouldn't wonder," said Robert. "Father says they infest old places – and this must be old if the sea was here thousands of years ago."

"Perhaps it is a snake," said Jane, shuddering.

"Oh, don't be silly!" said Anthea. "It's not a rat, it's MUCH bigger. And it's not a snake. It's got feet – I saw them – and fur! And I – it sounds silly, but it said something. It really did."

"What?" Cyril challenged.

"It said, 'You leave me alone.'"

But Cyril just observed that his sister must have gone off her nut, and he and Robert dug with spades while Anthea stood on the edge of the hole, jumping up and down. They dug carefully, and presently everyone could see that there really was something moving in the bottom of the Australian hole.

Then Anthea cried out, "I'm not afraid. Let me dig," and fell on her knees and began to scratch like a dog does when he has suddenly remembered where it was that he buried his bone.

"Oh, I felt fur," she cried, half laughing and half crying. "I did indeed!" when suddenly a dry husky voice in the sand made them all jump back, and their hearts jumped nearly as fast as they did.

"Leave me alone," it said. And now everyone heard the voice and looked at the others to see if they had too.

"But we want to see you," said Robert bravely.

"I wish you would come out," said Anthea, also taking courage.

"Oh, well – if that's your wish," the voice said, and the sand stirred and spun and scattered, and something brown and furry and fat came rolling

126

out into the hole and all the
sand fell off it, and it sat there
yawning and rubbing the
ends of its eyes with its hands.

"I believe I must have
dropped asleep," it said,
stretching itself.

The children stood
round the hole in a ring,
looking at the creature. Its eyes
were on long horns like a snail's
eyes, and it could move them
in and out like telescopes. It had ears
like a bat, and its body was shaped
like a spider's and covered with thick soft fur. Its
legs and arms were furry too, and it had hands
and feet rather like a monkey's.

"What on earth is it?" Jane said. "Shall we take
it home with us?"

The thing turned its strange eyes to look at her,
and said, "Does she always talk nonsense, or is it

the rubbish on her head that makes her silly?" and it looked scornfully at Jane's hat as it spoke.

"She doesn't mean to be silly," Anthea said. "None of us do, whatever you may think! Don't be frightened – we don't want to hurt you."

"Hurt ME!" it said. "ME frightened? Why, you talk as if I were nobody in particular." All its fur stood out like a cat's when it is going to fight.

"Well," said Anthea, still kindly, "perhaps if we knew who you are in particular we could think of something to say that wouldn't make you cross. Everything we've said so far seems to have. Who are you? Don't get angry! Because we don't know."

"You don't know?" it said. "Well, I knew the world had changed – but – well, really – do you mean to tell me seriously you don't know a Psammead when you see one?"

"A Sammyadd? That's Greek to me."

"So it is to everyone," said the creature sharply. "Well, in plain English, then, a SAND-FAIRY.

Don't you know a Sand-fairy when you see one?'

It looked so grieved and hurt that Jane hastened to say, "Of course I see you are, now. It's quite plain now one comes to look at you."

"You came to look at me, several sentences ago," it said crossly, beginning to curl up again in the sand.

"Oh – don't go away again! Do talk some more," Robert cried. "I didn't know you were a Sand-fairy, but I knew directly I saw you that you were much the wonderfullest thing I'd ever seen."

The Sand-fairy seemed a shade less disagreeable after this.

"It isn't talking I mind," it said, "as long as you're reasonably civil. But I'm not going to make polite conversation for you. If you talk nicely to me, I might answer you, I might not. Now say something."

Of course no one could think of anything to say, but at last Robert thought of 'How long have you lived here?' and he said it at once.

"Oh, ages – several thousand years," replied the Psammead.

"Tell us all about it. Do."

"It's all in books."

"You aren't!" Jane said. "Oh, tell us everything you can about yourself! We don't know anything about you, and you are so nice."

The Sand-fairy smoothed his long rat-like whiskers and smiled.

"Do please tell!" said the children all together.

It drew its eyes in and said, "How very sunny it is today – quite like the old times. It used to be very nearly all sand where I lived, and coal grew on the trees, and the periwinkles were as big as tea-trays – you can still find them now, they're turned into stone. We Sand-fairies used to live on the seashore, and the children would come along with their little flint-spades and flint-pails, and they would make castles for us to live in. That's thousands of years ago, but I hear that even now children still build castles on the sand. It's difficult to break yourself of a habit."

"But why did you stop living in the sandcastles?" asked Robert.

"It's a sad story," said the Psammead gloomily. "It was because they would build moats to the castles, and the nasty wet bubbling sea used to come in, and of course as soon as a Sand-fairy got wet it caught cold, and generally died. And so there got to be fewer and fewer."

"And did YOU get wet?" Robert enquired.

The Sand-fairy shuddered. "Only once," it said. "The very end of the twelfth hair of my top left whisker – I feel the place still if the weather is damp. It was only once, but it was quite more than enough for me.

"I went away as soon as the sun had dried my poor dear whisker. I scurried away to the back of the beach, and dug myself a house deep in warm dry sand, and there I've been ever since. And the sea changed its lodgings afterwards. And now I'm not going to tell you another thing."

"Just one more, please," said the children. "Can you give wishes now?"

"Of course," it said, "didn't I give you yours a few minutes ago? You said, 'I wish you'd come out,' and then I did."

"Oh, please, mayn't we have another?"

"Yes, but be quick about it. I'm tired of you."

I daresay you have often thought what you would do if you had three wishes given you, and have despised the old man and his wife in the black-pudding story, and felt certain that if you had the chance you could think of three really useful wishes without a moment's hesitation. These children had often talked this matter over, but, now the chance had suddenly come to them, they could not make up their minds.

"Quick," said the Sand-fairy crossly. No one could think of anything, only Anthea did manage to remember a private wish of her own and Jane's which they had never told the boys. She knew the boys would not think much of it – but still it was better than nothing.

"I wish we were all as beautiful as the day," she said in a great hurry.

The children looked at each other, but each could see that the others were not any better-looking than usual. The Psammead pushed out its eyes, and seemed to be holding its breath and swelling till it was twice as fat and furry as before. Suddenly it let its breath go in a long sigh.

"I'm really afraid I can't manage it," it said apologetically, 'I must be out of practice."

The children were horribly disappointed.

"Oh, DO try again!" they said.

"Well," said the Sand-fairy, "the fact is, I was keeping back a little strength to give the rest of you your wishes with. If you'll be contented with one wish a day amongst the lot of you I daresay I can screw myself up to it. Do you agree to that?"

"Yes, oh yes!'"said Jane and Anthea. The boys nodded. They did not really believe the Sand-fairy could do it.

It stretched out its eyes farther than ever, and swelled and swelled and swelled.

"I do hope it won't hurt itself," said Anthea.

"Or crack its skin," Robert said anxiously.

Everyone was very much relieved when the Sand-fairy, after getting so big that it almost filled up the hole in the sand, suddenly let out its breath and went back to its proper size.

"That's all right," it said, panting heavily. "It'll come easier tomorrow."

"Did it hurt much?" asked Anthea.

"Only my poor whisker, thank you," said he, "you're a kind and thoughtful child. Good day."

It scratched suddenly and fiercely with its hands and feet, and disappeared in the sand. Then the children looked at each other, and each child suddenly found itself alone with three perfect strangers, all radiantly beautiful.

The Three Wishes

From *More English Fairy Tales*
by Joseph Jacobs

Once upon a time, there lived a poor woodman in a great forest, and every day of his life he went out to fell timber. So one day he started out, and his wife filled his wallet and slung his bottle on his back, that he might have meat and drink in the forest. He had marked out a huge old oak, which he could chop into many good planks. When he had reached it, he took his axe and swung it round his head to fell the tree at one stroke. Suddenly, there stood before him a fairy who prayed and beseeched him to spare the tree.

He was dazed with wonderment and couldn't open his mouth to utter a word. When he found his tongue at last, he said, "I'll do as you ask."

"Thank you," answered the fairy, "and to show I'm grateful, I'll grant you three wishes, be they what they may." With that, the fairy vanished.

The woodman started for home. But the way was long, and the poor man was regularly dazed with the wonderful thing that had befallen him, and when he got home there was nothing in his head but the wish to sit down and rest.

"Isn't my supper ready yet?" said he to his wife.

"No, not for a couple of hours," said she.

"Ah!" groaned the woodman. "I wish I'd a good link of black pudding here before me."

No sooner had he said it, when clatter, clatter, rustle, rustle, what should come down the chimney but a link of the finest black pudding.

"What's all this?" his wife said, bewildered.

Then the woodman remembered the fairy and told his wife what had happened.

"Oh, you are a fool," she burst out. "I wish the pudding were on your nose, I do indeed."

Before you could say 'Jack Robinson', a link of black pudding appeared on the woodman's nose.

He gave a pull, but it stuck, and she gave a pull, but it stuck, and they both pulled till they had nearly pulled the nose off, but it stuck fast.

"What's to be done now?" said he.

"Well... I suppose it doesn't look all that bad," replied his wife.

Then the woodman saw that if he wished, he should wish quickly, and wish he did, that the black pudding might come off his nose. Well! There it lay in a dish on the table, and if the woodman and his wife didn't ride in a golden coach, or dress in silk and satin, why, they had at least as fine a black pudding for their supper as anyone would want.

The Magical Mug

An extract from *The King of the Golden River*
by John Ruskin

*Three brothers, Hans, Schwartz, and Gluck (the youngest), are
goldsmiths who live in Treasure Valley, high up in the mountains
of Austria. The two elder brothers are unpleasant and wicked, and
one day they cruelly decide to melt down Gluck's only precious
possession – a golden mug that has the face of a bearded
man upon it – and they put it in the furnace...*

It was just at the close of the day, and, when the
goldsmith Gluck sat down at the window, he
saw the rocks of the mountain-tops, all crimson
and purple with the sunset, and there were bright
tongues of fiery cloud burning and quivering
about them, and the river, brighter than

everything around it, fell, in a waving column of pure gold, from precipice to precipice, with a broad rainbow stretched across it, flushing and fading alternately in the wreaths of spray.

"Ah!" said Gluck aloud. "If that river was really all gold, what a nice thing it would be!"

"No, it wouldn't, Gluck," said a clear, metallic voice, close at his ear.

"Bless me, what's that?" exclaimed Gluck, jumping up. There was nobody there. He looked round the room, and under the table, and a great many times behind him, but there was certainly nobody there, and he sat down again at the window. This time he didn't speak, but he couldn't help wishing again that the river was really all gold.

"Not at all, my boy," said the same voice, louder than before.

"Bless me!" said Gluck again. "What is that?" He looked again into all the corners and cupboards, and then began turning round and round, as fast as he could, in the middle of the room, thinking there was somebody behind him, when the same voice struck again on his ear. It was singing now very merrily "Lala-lira-la" – no words, only a soft melody. Gluck looked out of the window. No, it was certainly in the house. Upstairs and downstairs. No, it was certainly in that very room. "Lala-lira-la."

All at once it struck Gluck that it sounded louder near the furnace. He ran to the opening and looked in. Yes, he saw right, it seemed to be coming, not only out of the furnace, but out of the pot. He uncovered it, and ran back in a great fright, for the pot was certainly singing! He stood in the farthest corner of the room, with his hands up, and his mouth open, for a minute or two.

Then the singing stopped and the voice said, "Hello!"

Gluck was too utterly shocked to answer.

"Hello! Gluck, my boy," came the voice again. This time, Gluck summoned all his energies, walked straight up to the furnace and looked in. There, in the crucible, was the gold of his mug, all melted. But on the surface of the golden liquid lay the red nose and the sharp eyes of his old friend on the mug, a thousand times redder and sharper than ever he had seen them in his life.

"Come, Gluck, my boy," said the voice out of the molten gold, "I'm all right; pour me out."

But Gluck was too much astonished to do anything of the kind.

"Pour me out, I say," said the voice, gruffly. Still Gluck couldn't move.

"Will you pour me out?" said the voice. "I'm hot."

Gluck finally sprang into action, took hold of the crucible, and sloped it so as to pour out the contents. At first liquid gold and steam poured out, but after a moment there emerged, first the well-known head of his friend the

142

mug, then a pair of arms stuck akimbo, then some coat-tails, and finally a pair of pretty little yellow legs. And standing there before him on the floor was a golden dwarf, about a foot and a half high.

"That's right!" said the dwarf, stretching out first his legs, and then his arms, and then shaking his head up and down, and as far round as it would go, apparently to see if he was quite correctly put together, while Gluck stood in speechless amazement.

The dwarf was dressed in a slashed doublet of gleaming spun gold. Over this, his hair and beard fell almost to the ground, in a wave of curls. The features of his face were rather coarse and even coppery in colour, which made the dwarf look as though he was a very determined and fiery-tempered person.

When the dwarf had finished checking himself over, he turned his small, sharp eyes full on Gluck, and stared at him. "No, it wouldn't, Gluck, my boy," said the little man.

This was certainly rather an abrupt way to begin conversation. Gluck supposed that it might be a comment on his earlier thoughts about wishing that the river were really gold. But whether it was or wasn't, Gluck wasn't about to argue with the dwarf.

"Wouldn't it, sir?" said Gluck, very mildly and submissively indeed.

"No," said the dwarf, conclusively. "No, it would not." And saying that, he pulled his cap hard over his brows, and took three steps down the room, turned and took three steps back, lifting his legs very high, and setting them down very hard.

This pause gave time for Gluck to collect his thoughts. "Sir," he asked, rather hesitatingly, "were you my mug?"

On which the little man span round, walked straight up to Gluck, and drew himself up to his full height. "I," said the little man, "am the king of the Golden River." Whereupon he turned about again, and paced up and down once more.

Gluck thought he should say something. "I hope Your Majesty is very well?" he asked.

"Listen!" said the little man, not bothering to reply. "I am the king of what you mortals call the Golden River. I had been enchanted into the shape of a mug by a stronger, evil king, from whose wicked spell you have just freed me. I know you are a good lad, unlike your wicked brothers, and I would like to help you, so listen to what I say.

"Whoever shall climb to the top of that mountain from which you see the Golden River spring, and shall cast into the stream at its source three drops of holy water, for him, and for him only, the river shall turn to gold. But no one failing in his first attempt can have another go, and anyone who casts unholy water into the river will become a black stone."

So saying, the king of the Golden River turned away, and deliberately walked into the centre of the hottest flame of the furnace. His figure became red, white, transparent, dazzling – a blaze of intense light that rose, trembled, and disappeared. The king of the Golden River had evaporated.

"Oh!" cried poor Gluck, running to look up the chimney after him, "Oh dear, dear, dear me! My mug! My mug! My mug!"

An Unexpected Opening

An extract from *The Brass Bottle*
by F Anstey

*Horace Ventimore is a young man living in Victorian
times in London. He buys an antique bottle, which turns
out to be much more than he had bargained for...*

Horace went up to his sitting-room. It was
quite dark and he had to light his oil-
lamps. After he had done so, the first object he
saw was the long-necked jar that he had bought
that afternoon, and which stood on the floor near
the mantelpiece.

"It's uglier than I thought," he said to himself.
"What an idiot I was to waste money on it! I

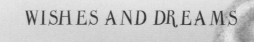

wonder if there is anything inside? I'll
have to find out before I go to bed."

He grasped it and tried to twist the
cap off, but it remained firm, which was
not surprising, seeing that it was
thickly coated with a crust like
cooled, hard lava from a volcano.

"I must get some of that off first,
and then try again," he decided, and
after foraging downstairs, he returned
with a hammer and chisel, with which
he chipped away the crust till
the line of the cap was
revealed, together with a
clumsy-looking metal
knob that seemed to be a
catch. He fiddled with this
for some

time, and again attempted to wrench off
the lid. Then he gripped the vessel between
his knees and used all his strength. The cap
was beginning to give way, very slightly.
One last wrench – and it came off in his
hand so suddenly that he fell backwards and
hit his head on the floor with a thump.

He had a vague impression of the
bottle lying on its side, with dense
volumes of hissing smoke pouring out
of its mouth and towering up in a
gigantic column to the ceiling. He
was also aware of a strong smell,
before he fainted clean away.

When he opened his eyes the
room was still thick with smoke. As
it cleared, Horace saw the figure of a
stranger – an elderly man wearing an
Eastern robe and headdress of a
dark-green hue. He stood there with
uplifted hands, loudly uttering

149

something in a strange language.

Horace, being still somewhat dazed, felt no surprise. He thought that his landlady must have rented out the next-door apartment at last. His new neighbour must have noticed the smoke and rushed in to offer help.

"Awfully good of you to come in, sir," he said, as he scrambled to his feet. "I don't know what's happened exactly, but there's no harm done. I dare say you've been rather startled. So was I, when I opened that bottle."

"Tell me," pronounced the stranger in a booming voice, "was it thy hand that removed the seal, O young man of kindness and good works?"

"I certainly did open it," said Horace, "though I don't know where the kindness comes in – for I've no notion what was inside the thing."

"I was inside it," said the curious stranger, calmly.

"So you were inside that bottle, were you?"

said Horace. "How amazing!" He realized that his new neighbour must be slightly mad, and it would probably be best to play along with him.

"Dost thou doubt that I speak truth? I tell thee that I have been confined in that accursed vessel for countless centuries. Know that he who now addresses thee is Fakrash-el-Aamash, one of the Green Jinn. And I dwelt in the Palace of the Mountain of the Clouds above the City of Babel in the Garden of Irem, which thou doubtless knowest by repute?"

"I fancy I have heard of it," said Horace, as if it were an address in the phone book. "Delightful neighbourhood."

"But now, by thy means, my deliverance hath been accomplished. Demand whatever you wish, therefore, and thou shalt receive."

"My dear Mr Fakrash," Horace replied, "I've done nothing – nothing at all – and if I had, I couldn't possibly accept any reward for it."

'Tomorrow,' thought Horace, 'I'll speak to the

landlady, and get her to send for a doctor and have this old boy put under proper care – he really isn't fit to live on his own!'

"The hour is late and I will leave thee awhile," proclaimed the stranger. "But I will return and serve you. May thy days be ever fortunate!" And as he finished speaking, he seemed, to Horace's speechless amazement, to slip through the wall behind him. At all events, he had left the room somehow – and Horace found himself alone.

He rubbed the back of his head, which began to be painful. "He can't really have vanished through the wall," he said to himself. " I must be over-excited this evening – hardly surprising, with all that has happened. The best thing I can do is to go to bed at once."

Which he accordingly proceeded to do.

The Lad Who Went to the North Wind

From *Popular Tales from the Norse*
by Sir George Webbe Dasent

Once upon on a time there was an old widow who had one son, and as she was poorly and weak, her son had to go up into the safe to fetch meal for cooking. But when he got outside the safe, and was just going down the steps, there came the North Wind, puffing and blowing, caught up the meal, and so away with it through the air. Then the lad went back into the safe for more, but when he came out again on the steps, the North Wind came again and carried off the meal with a puff, and, more than that, he did so the third time.

At this the lad got very angry. He determined to look up the North Wind and ask for his meal back. So off he went, but the way was long, and he walked and walked, but at last he came to the North Wind's house.

"Good day!" said the lad. "Thank you for coming to see us yesterday."

"Good day!" answered the North Wind, in a voice that was loud and gruff. "And thanks for coming to see me. What do you want?"

"I only wished to ask

154

you to be so good as to let me have back that
meal that you took from me," said the lad, "for we
haven't very much to live on, and if you're to go
on snapping up the last morsel we have, there'll
be nothing for it but for us to starve."

"I haven't got your meal," said the North
Wind, "but if you are in such need, I'll give you a
cloth that will get you everything you wish, if you
only say, 'Cloth, spread yourself, and serve up all
kind of good dishes!'"

With this the lad was well content.

As the way was so long he couldn't get home in
one day, so he turned into an inn on the way, and
when they were going to sit down to supper he

laid the cloth on a table that stood in the corner, and said, "Cloth, spread yourself, and serve up all kinds of good dishes." He had scarce said so before the cloth did as it was bid, and all who stood by thought it a fine thing, but most of all the landlady. So, when all were fast asleep at dead of night, she took the lad's cloth, and put another in its stead, just like the one he had got from the North Wind, but which couldn't so much as serve up a bit of dry bread.

When the lad woke, he took his cloth and went off with it, and that day he got home to his mother. "Now," said he, "I've been to the North

Wind's house, and a good fellow he is, for he gave me this cloth, and when I only say to it, 'Cloth, spread yourself, and serve up all kinds of good dishes,' I get any sort of food I please."

Next morning off went the lad, and when he got home to his mother, he said, "After all, the North Wind is a jolly fellow, for now he has given me a ram that can coin golden ducats if I only say 'Ram, ram! Make money!'"

"All very true, I daresay," said his mother, "but I shan't believe any such stuff until I see the ducats made for myself."

"Ram, ram! Make money!" said the lad, but if the ram made anything, it wasn't money.

So the lad went back again to the North Wind, and blew him up, and said the ram was worth nothing, and he must have his rights for the meal.

"Well!" said the North Wind. "I've nothing else to give you, except for that old stick in the corner yonder, but it is a stick of that kind that if you wish, 'Stick, stick! Lay on!' it lays on till you say, 'Stick, stick! Now stop!'"

As the way was long, the lad turned in this night too to the landlord, but as he could pretty well guess how things stood as to the cloth and the ram, he lay down at once on the bench and began to snore, as if he were asleep.

Now the landlord, who easily saw that the stick must be worth something, hunted up one that was like it, and when he heard the lad snore, was going to change the two. But, just as the landlord was about to take it, the lad bawled out, "Stick, stick! Lay on!"

So the stick began to beat the landlord, till he jumped over chairs, and tables, and benches, and yelled and roared, "Oh my! Oh my! Bid the stick be still, else it will beat me to death, and you shall have back both your cloth and your ram."

When the lad thought the landlord had got enough, he said, "Stick, stick! Now stop!"

Then he took the cloth and put it into his pocket, and went home with his stick in his hand, leading the ram by a cord round its horns.

So he got his rights for the meal he had lost.

The Council with the Munchkins 162

The Mines 175

The Buried Moon 186

Do You Believe in Fairies? 209

The Giant Builder 196

MAGICAL
PLACES

Arndt's Night Underground 216

Shipwreck on Lilliput 228

A Grin Without a Cat 238

The Deliverers of their Country 244

The Council with the Munchkins

An extract from *The Wonderful Wizard of Oz*
by L Frank Baum

Dorothy sat up and noticed that the house was not moving. Nor was it dark, for the bright sunshine came in at the window, flooding the little room. She sprang from her bed and, with Toto at her heels, ran and opened the door.

The little girl gave a cry of amazement and looked about her, her eyes growing bigger and bigger at the wonderful sights she saw.

The cyclone had set the house down very gently – for a cyclone – in the midst of a country of marvellous beauty. There were lovely patches of grass all about, with stately trees bearing rich and luscious fruits. Banks of gorgeous flowers were on every hand, and birds with rare and brilliant plumage sang and fluttered in the trees and bushes. A little way off was a small brook, rushing and sparkling along between green banks, and murmuring in a voice very grateful to a little girl who had lived so long on the dry, grey prairies.

While she stood looking eagerly at the strange and beautiful sights, she noticed coming towards her a group of the queerest people she had ever seen. They were not as big as the grown folk she had always been used to, but neither were they very small. In fact, they seemed about as tall as Dorothy, who was a well-grown child for her age, although they were, so far as looks go, many years older.

Three were men and one a woman, and all were oddly dressed. They wore round hats that rose to a small point a foot above their heads,

with little bells around the brims
that tinkled sweetly as they moved.
The hats of the men were blue, the
little woman's hat was white, and
she wore a white gown that hung in
pleats from her shoulders. Over it
were sprinkled little stars that
glistened in the sun like diamonds.
The men were dressed in blue, of the
same shade as their hats, and wore
well-polished boots. The men,
Dorothy thought, were about as old as Uncle
Henry, for two of them had beards. But the little
woman was doubtless much older. Her face was
covered with wrinkles, her hair was nearly white,
and she walked rather stiffly.

When these people drew near the house where
Dorothy was standing in the doorway, they
paused and whispered among themselves, as if
afraid to come farther. But the little old woman
walked up to Dorothy, made a low bow and said,

in a sweet voice, "You are welcome, most noble Sorceress, to the land of the Munchkins. We are so grateful to you for having killed the Wicked Witch of the East, and for setting our people free from bondage."

Dorothy listened to this speech with wonder. What could the little woman possibly mean by calling her a sorceress, and saying she had killed the Wicked Witch of the East?

Dorothy was an innocent, harmless little girl, who had been carried by a cyclone many miles from home, and she knew very well that she had never killed anything in all her life.

But the little woman evidently expected her to answer, so Dorothy said, with hesitation, "You are very kind, but there must be some mistake. I have not killed anything."

"Your house did, anyway," replied the little old woman, with a laugh, "and that is the same thing.

She pointed to the
corner of the house.

"There are her two feet, still sticking out from
under a block of wood."

Dorothy looked, and gave a little cry of fright.
There, indeed, just under the corner of the great
beam the house rested on, two feet were sticking
out, shod in silver shoes with pointed toes.

"Oh, dear! Oh, dear!" cried Dorothy, clasping
her hands together in great dismay. "The house
must have fallen on her. Whatever shall we do?"

"There is nothing to be done," said the little

woman calmly.

"But who was she?" asked Dorothy.

"She was the Wicked Witch of the East, as I said," answered the little woman. "She has held all the Munchkins in bondage for many years, making them slave for her night and day. Now they are all set free, and are grateful to you for the favour."

"Who are the Munchkins?" enquired Dorothy.

"They are the people who live in this land of the East where the Wicked Witch ruled."

"Are you a Munchkin?" asked Dorothy.

"No, but I am their friend, although I live in the land of the North. When they discovered that the Witch of the East was dead the Munchkins sent a swift messenger to me, and I came at once. I am the Witch of the North."

"Oh, gracious!" cried Dorothy. "Are you a real witch?"

"Yes, indeed," answered the little woman. "But I am a good witch, and the people love me.

I am not as powerful as the Wicked Witch was who ruled here, or I should have set the people free myself."

"But I thought all witches were wicked," said the girl, who was half frightened at facing a real witch.

"Oh, no, that is a great mistake. There were only four witches in all the Land of Oz, and two of them, those who live in the North and the South, are good witches. I know this is true, for I am one of them myself, and cannot be mistaken. Those who dwelled in the East and the West were, indeed, wicked witches, but now that you have killed one of them, there is but one Wicked Witch in all the Land of Oz – the one who lives in the West."

"But," said Dorothy, after a moment's thought, "Aunt Em has told me that the witches were all dead – years and years ago."

"And who is Aunt Em?" enquired the little old woman, gently.

"She is my aunt and she lives in Kansas – where I came from."

The Witch of the North seemed to think for a time, with her head bowed and her eyes upon the ground. Then she looked up and said, "I do not know where Kansas is, for I have never heard that country mentioned before. But tell me, is it a civilized country?"

"Oh, yes," replied Dorothy.

"Then that accounts for it. In the civilized countries I believe there are no witches left, nor wizards, nor sorceresses, nor magicians. But, you see, the Land of Oz has never been civilized, for we are cut off from all the rest of the world. Therefore we still have witches and wizards among us."

"Who are the wizards?" asked Dorothy.

"Oz himself is the Great Wizard," answered the Witch, sinking her voice to a whisper. "He is more powerful than all the rest of us together. He lives in the City of Emeralds."

Dorothy was going to ask another question, but just then the Munchkins, who had been standing silently by, gave a loud shout and pointed to the corner of the house where the Wicked Witch had been lying.

"What is it?" asked the little old woman, and looked, and began to laugh. The feet of the dead Witch had disappeared entirely, and nothing was left but the silver shoes.

"She was so old," explained the Witch of the North, "that she dried up quickly in the sun. That is the end of her. But the silver shoes are yours, and you shall have them to wear." She reached down and picked up the shoes, and after shaking the dust out of them handed them to Dorothy.

"The Witch of the East was proud of those silver shoes," said one of the Munchkins, "and there is some charm connected with them, but what it is we never knew."

Dorothy carried the shoes into the house and placed them on the table. Then she came out again to the Munchkins and said, "I am anxious to get back to my aunt and uncle, for I am sure they will worry about me. Can you help me find my way?"

The Munchkins and the Witch first looked at one another, and then at Dorothy, and then they shook their heads.

"At the East, not far from here," said one, "there is a great desert, and none could live to cross it."

"It is the same at the South," said another, "for I have been there and seen it. The South is the country of the Quadlings."

"I am told," said the third man, "that it is the same at the West. And that country, where the Winkies live, is ruled by the Wicked Witch of the West, who would make you her slave if you passed her way."

"The North is my home," said the old lady, "and at its edge is the same great desert that surrounds this Land of Oz. I'm afraid, my dear, you will have to live with us."

Dorothy began to sob at this, for she felt lonely among all these strange people. Her tears seemed to grieve the kind-hearted Munchkins, for they immediately took out their handkerchiefs and began to weep also. As for the little old woman, she took off her cap and balanced the point on the end of her nose, while she counted "One, two, three" in a solemn voice. At once the cap changed to a slate, on which was written in big, white chalk marks:

LET DOROTHY GO TO THE CITY OF EMERALDS.

The little old woman took the slate from her nose, and having read the words on it, asked, "Is your name Dorothy, my dear?"

"Yes," answered the child, looking up and drying her tears.

"Then you must go to the City of Emeralds. Perhaps Oz will help you."

"Where is this city?" asked Dorothy.

"It is exactly in the centre of the country, and is ruled by Oz, the Great Wizard I told you of."

"Is he a good man?" enquired the girl anxiously.

"He is a good Wizard. Whether he is a man or not I cannot tell, for I have never seen him."

"How can I get there?" asked Dorothy.

"You must walk. It is a long journey, through a country that is sometimes pleasant and sometimes dark and terrible. However, I will use all the magic arts I know to keep you from harm."

"Won't you go with me?" pleaded the girl, who had begun to look upon the little old woman as her only friend.

"I can't do that," she replied, "but I will give you my kiss, and no one will dare injure a person who has been kissed by the Witch of the North."

She came close to Dorothy and kissed her gently on the forehead. Where her lips touched the girl they left a round, shining mark.

"The road to the City of Emeralds is paved with yellow brick," said the Witch, "so you cannot miss it. When you get to Oz do not be afraid of him, but tell your story and ask him to help. Goodbye, my dear."

The Munchkins bowed low and wished her a pleasant journey, then walked away through the trees. The Witch gave Dorothy a friendly nod, whirled around on her left heel three times, and disappeared, much to the surprise of Toto, who barked after her loudly when she had gone, but had been afraid even to growl while she stood by.

But Dorothy, knowing her to be a witch, had expected her to disappear in just that way, and was not surprised in the least.

The Mines

An extract from *The Princess and the Goblin*
by George MacDonald

*A young princess called Irene knows nothing of the menacing
goblins who live under the nearby mountains – until one day she
and her nanny stay out late and are chased by a hideous creature.
They are rescued by a boy called Curdie, who knows all about goblins
because he works in the mountain mines. One night, when Curdie is
working alone, he comes across yet more of them, and decides to
follow them to see what they are plotting...*

The work was hard, for it is very warm
underground, but some of the miners,
when they wanted to earn a little more money for
a particular purpose, would stop behind the rest
and work all night. You could not tell night from

day down there, for no light of the sun ever came into those gloomy regions. Some who had thus remained behind during the night, although certain there were none of their companions at work, would declare the next morning that they heard, every time they halted for a moment to take breath, a tap-tapping all about them, as if the mountain were then more full of miners than ever it was during the day, and some in consequence would never stay overnight, for all knew those were the sounds of the goblins.

They worked only at night, for the miners' night was the goblins' day. Indeed, most of the miners were afraid of the goblins, for there were stories about what the goblins would do to any miners they found. The more courageous of them, however, stayed in the mine all night again and again, and although they had several times encountered a few stray goblins, had never yet failed in driving them away. The chief defence against them was poetry, for they hated verse of every kind, and some kinds they could not endure at all. I suspect they could not make any themselves, and that was why they disliked it so much.

At all events, those who were most afraid of them were those who could neither make verses themselves nor remember the verses that other people made for them, while those who were never afraid were those who could make verses for themselves, for although there were certain old rhymes that were very effectual, yet it was well known that a new rhyme, if of the right sort, was even more distasteful to them, and therefore more effectual in putting them to flight.

That night, Curdie was the only one who remained in the mine. At about six o'clock the rest went away, everyone bidding him good night, and telling him to take care of himself.

For some time he worked away briskly, throwing all the ore he had dug on one side behind him, to be ready for carrying out in the morning. He heard a good deal of goblin-tapping, but it all sounded far away in the hill, and he paid it little heed. Towards midnight he began to feel rather hungry, so he dropped his pickaxe, got out a lump of bread that in the morning he had laid in a damp hole in the rock, sat down on a heap of ore, and ate his supper. Then he leaned back for five minutes' rest before beginning his work again, and laid his head against the rock.

He had not kept the position for one minute before he heard something that made him sharpen his ears. It sounded like a voice inside the rock. After a while he heard it again. It was a goblin voice – there could be no doubt about that –

and this time he could make out the words.

"Hadn't we better be moving?" it said.

A rougher and deeper voice replied, "There's no hurry. That wretched little mole won't be through tonight, if he works ever so hard. He's not by any means at the thinnest place."

Curdie realized they were wrong – it could be but a thin partition that now separated them. If only he could get through in time to follow the goblins as they retreated! A few blows would doubtless be sufficient – just where his ear now lay, but if he attempted to strike there with his pickaxe, he would only put the goblins on their guard and hasten their departure. He therefore began to feel the wall with his hands, and soon found that some of the stones were loose enough to be drawn out with little noise. Laying hold of a large one with both his hands, he drew it gently out, and let it down softly.

"What was that noise?" said the older voice.

Curdie blew out his light, lest it should shine

through and give him away.

"Maybe it was a stone carried down by the brook inside," said a voice that Curdie guessed must be a female goblin.

"Perhaps," said the younger voice.

Curdie kept quite still. After a little while, hearing nothing but the sounds of the goblin family's preparations for departure, mingled with an occasional word of direction, he put in his hand to feel. It went in a good way and touched something soft. He had but a moment to feel it over, it was so quickly withdrawn – it was a goblin foot! The owner of it gave a cry of fright.

"What's the matter, Helfer?" asked his mother.

"A beast came out of the wall and licked my foot."

"Nonsense! There are no
wild beasts in our country," said his
father.

"But it was, father. I felt it."

"Nonsense, I say."

"But I did feel it, father."

"I tell you to hold your
tongue."

Curdie suppressed his
laughter, and lay still as a
mouse – but no stiller, for
every moment he kept
nibbling away with his fingers at
the edges of the hole. He was slowly making it
bigger, for here the rock had been very much
shattered with the blasting.

There seemed to be a good many in the family,
to judge from the mass of confused talk that now
and then came through the hole, but when all
were speaking together, and just as if they had
bottle-brushes – each at least one – in their

throats, it was not easy to make out much that was said. At length he heard once more what the father goblin was saying.

"Now, then," he said, "get your bundles on your backs. Make haste. I must go to the meeting at the palace tonight. When that's over, we can come back and clear out the last of the things before our enemies return in the morning. Now light your torches and come along."

A sound of many soft feet followed, but soon ceased. Then Curdie flew at the hole like a tiger, and tore and pulled. The sides gave way, and it was soon large enough for him to crawl through. He would not betray himself by rekindling his lamp, but the torches of the retreating company, which he found departing in a straight line up a long avenue from the door of their cave, threw back light enough to afford him to see.

He darted after them like a greyhound. When he reached the corner and looked cautiously round, he saw them again at some distance down another long passage. None of the galleries he saw that night bore signs of the work of man – or of goblin either. Stalactites, far older than the mines, hung from their roofs, and their floors were rough with boulders and large, round stones, showing that water must have once run there.

He waited again at this corner till they had disappeared round the next, and so followed them a long way through one passage after another. The passages grew more and more lofty, and were more and more covered in the roof with shining stalactites.

In a moment or two, keeping after the goblins round another corner, he started back in amazement. He was at the entrance of a magnificent cavern, of an oval shape, once probably a huge natural reservoir of water. It rose to a tremendous height, but the roof was composed of such shining materials, and the multitude of torches carried by the goblins who crowded the floor lighted up the place so brilliantly, that Curdie could see to the top quite well. But he had no idea how immense the place was until his eyes had got accustomed to it, which was not for a good many minutes. The rough projections on the walls, and the shadows thrown upwards from them by the torches, made the sides of the chamber look as if they were crowded with statues upon brackets and pedestals, reaching in irregular tiers from floor to roof. The walls themselves were, in many parts, of gloriously shining substances, some of them gorgeously coloured besides, which powerfully contrasted with the shadows.

It was the great palace of the goblins.

And at the far end, high above the heads of the multitude, sitting on a terrace-like ledge, was the goblin king and his court.

The Buried Moon

From *Tales of Wonder Every Child Should Know*
by Kate Douglas Wiggin and
Nora Archibald Smith

*L*ong ago, the Carland was all in bogs, great pools of black water, and creeping trickles of green water, and squishy mools that squirted when you stepped on them. The Moon up yonder shone just as she does now, and when she shone she lighted up the bogpools, so that one could walk about almost as safe as in the day. But when she didn't shine, out came the Things that dwelled in the darkness and went about seeking to do evil and harm – Bogles and Crawling Horrors, all came out when the Moon didn't shine.

Well, the Moon heard of this, and being kind and good – as she surely is, shining for us in the night instead of taking her natural rest – she was troubled. "I'll see for myself, I will," said she, "maybe it's not so bad as folks make out."

Sure enough, at the month's end down she stepped, wrapped up in a black cloak, and a black hood over her yellow shining hair. Straight she went to the bog edge and looked about her. Water here and water there, waving tussocks and trembling mools, and great black snags all twisted and bent. Before her all was dark – dark but for the glimmer of the stars in the pools, and the light that came from her own white feet, stealing out of her black cloak.

The Moon drew her cloak faster about her and trembled, but she wouldn't go back without seeing all there was to be seen, so on she went, stepping as light as the wind in summer from tuft to tuft between the muddy, gurgling water holes. Just as she came near a big black pool her foot slipped and she was close to tumbling in. She grabbed with both hands at a snag nearby, to steady herself with, but as she touched it, it twined itself round her wrists, like a pair of handcuffs, and gripped her so that she couldn't move. She pulled and twisted and fought, but it was no good. She was stuck, and must stay stuck.

Presently as she stood trembling in the dark, wondering if help would come, she heard something calling in the distance, calling, calling, and then dying away with a sob, till the marshes were full of a pitiful crying sound. Then she heard steps floundering along, squishing in the mud and slipping on the tufts, and in the darkness she saw a white face with great feared eyes.

It was a man strayed in the bogs. Dazed with fear he struggled on towards the flickering light that looked like help and safety. And when the poor Moon saw that he was coming nearer and nearer to the deep hole, farther and farther from the path, she was so mad and so sorry that she struggled and fought and pulled harder than ever. And though she couldn't get loose she twisted and turned, till her black hood fell back off her shining yellow hair, and the beautiful light that came from it drove away the darkness.

Oh, but the man cried with joy to see the light again. And at once all evil things fled back into the dark corners, for they cannot abide the light. So he could see where he was, and where the path was, and how he could get out of the marsh. And he was in such haste to get away from the Quicks, and Bogles, and Things that dwelled there, that he scarce looked at the brave light that came from the beautiful shining yellow hair, streaming out over the black cloak and falling to the water at his feet. And the Moon herself was so taken up with saving him, and with rejoicing that he was back on the right path, that she clean forgot that she needed help herself, and that she was held fast by the black snag.

So off he went, spent and gasping, and stumbling and sobbing with joy, flying for his life out of the terrible bogs. Then it came over the Moon, that she would like to go with him. So she pulled and fought as if she were mad, till she fell on her knees, spent with tugging, at the foot of the snag. And as she lay there, gasping for breath, the black hood fell forward over her head. So out went the blessed light and back came the darkness, with all its Evil Things, with a screech and a howl. They came crowding round her, mocking and snatching and beating, shrieking with rage and spite, and swearing and snarling, for they knew her to be their old enemy, that drove them back into the corners, and kept them from working their wicked wills.

They caught hold of her, with horrid bony fingers, and laid her deep in the water at the foot of the snag. And the Bogles fetched a strange big stone and rolled it on top of her, to keep her from rising. And they told two of the Will-o-the-wykes to take turns in watching on the black snag, to see that she lay safe and still, and couldn't get out to spoil their sport. And there lay the poor Moon, dead and buried in the bog till someone would set her loose – and who'd know where to look for her?

Well, the days passed, and it was the time for the new moon's coming, and the folk looked about, for the Moon was a good friend to the marsh folk, and they were main glad when the dark time was gone, and the paths were safe again, and the Evil Things were driven back by the blessed Light into the darkness and the waterholes.

But days and days passed, and the new Moon never came, and the nights were dark, and the Evil Things were worse than ever. And still the days went on, and the new Moon never came. The poor folk were strangely feared and amazed.

One day, as they sat in the inn, a man from the far end of the bog lands was smoking and listening to the talk about the Moon, when all at once he sat up and slapped his knee. "I'd clean forgot, but I reckon I know where the Moon be!" he said, and he told them of how he was lost in the bogs, and how, when he was nearly dead with fright, the light shone out, and he found the path and got home safe.

So come the next night in the darklings, out

they went all together, everyone feeling, as you can believe, fearful and scared. And they stumbled and stottered along the paths into the midst of the bogs. They saw nothing, though they heard sighings and flutterings in their ears, and felt cold wet fingers touching them, but all together, looking around, while they came near to the pool beside the great snag, where the Moon lay buried. And all at once they stopped, quaking and dazed and scared, for there was the great stone, half in, half out of the water, for all the world like a big strange coffin, and at the head was the black snag, stretching out its two arms in a dark gruesome cross, and on it a tiny light flickered, like a dying candle. And they all knelt down in the mud, and said, "Our Lord."

Then they went nearer, and took hold of the big stone, and shoved it up, and afterward they said that for one minute they saw a strange and beautiful face looking up at them out of the black water, but the Light came so quick and so white and shining, that they stepped back, dazed by it, and the very next minute, when they could see again, there was the full Moon in the sky, bright and beautiful and kind as ever, shining and smiling down at them, and making the bogs and the paths as clear as day, and stealing into the very corners, as though she'd have driven the darkness and the Bogles clean away if she could.

The Giant Builder

A Norse tale from *In the Days of Giants*
by Abbie Farwell Brown

Ages and ages ago, when the world was
first made, the gods decided to build
a beautiful city high above the heavens, the most
glorious and wonderful city that ever was known.
Asgard was to be its name, and it was to stand on
Ida Plain under the shade of Yggdrasil, the great
tree whose roots were underneath the earth.

First of all they built a house with a silver roof,
where there were seats for all the twelve chiefs. In
the midst, and high above the rest, was the
wonder throne of Odin the All-Father, whence

he could see everything that happened in the sky or on the earth or in the sea. Next they made a fair house for Queen Frigg and her lovely daughters. Then they built a smithy, with great hammers, tongs, anvils, and bellows, where the gods could work at their favourite trade, the making of beautiful things out of gold, which they did so well that folk name that time the Golden Age. Afterwards, as they had more leisure, they built separate houses for all the gods, each more beautiful than the preceding, for of course they were continually growing more skilful.

They saved Father Odin's palace until the last, for they meant this to be the largest and the most splendid of all. Gladsheim, the home of joy, was the name of Odin's house, and it was built all of gold, set in the midst of a wood whereof the trees had leaves of ruddy gold – like an autumn-gilded forest. For the safety of All-Father it was surrounded by a roaring river and by a high picket fence, and there was a great courtyard within. The glory of Gladsheim was its wondrous hall, radiant with gold, the most lovely room that time has ever seen. Valhalla, the Hall of Heroes, was the name of it, and it was roofed with the mighty shields of warriors. The ceiling was made of interlacing spears, and there was a portal at the west end before which hung a great grey wolf, while over him a fierce eagle hovered. The hall

was so huge that it had five hundred and forty gates, through each of which eight hundred men could march abreast. Indeed, there needed to be room, for this was the hall where every morning Odin received all the brave warriors who had died in battle on the earth below, and there were many heroes in those days. A happy life it was for the heroes, and a happy life for all who dwelled in Asgard, for this was before trouble had come among the gods, following the mischief of Loki.

This is how the trouble began. From the beginning of time, the giants had been unfriendly to the gods, because the giants were older and huger and more wicked. Besides, they were jealous because the good gods were fast gaining more wisdom and power than the giants had ever known. The giants hated the gods, and tried all in their power to injure them and the men of the earth below, whom the gods loved and cared for. The gods had already built a wall around Midgard, the world of men, to keep the giants

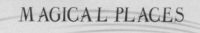

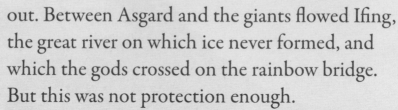

out. Between Asgard and the giants flowed Ifing, the great river on which ice never formed, and which the gods crossed on the rainbow bridge. But this was not protection enough.

So the word went forth in Asgard. "We must build a fortress against the giants – the hugest, strongest, finest fortress that ever was built."

Now one day soon after, there came a mighty man stalking up

the rainbow bridge that led to Asgard city.

"Who goes there!" cried Heimdal the watchman, whose eyes were so keen that he could easily see for one hundred miles around, and whose ears were so sharp that he could hear the grass growing in the meadow and the wool on the backs of the sheep. "Who goes there! There is no person who may enter Asgard if I say no."

"I am a builder," said the stranger, who was a huge fellow with sleeves rolled up to show the iron muscles of his arms. "I am a builder of strong towers, and I have heard that the folk of Asgard need one to help them raise a fair fortress in their city."

Heimdal looked at the stranger narrowly, for there was something about him that his sharp eyes did not like. But he made no answer, only blew on his golden horn, which was so loud that it sounded through all the world. At this signal all the gods came running to the rainbow bridge, from wherever they happened to be, to find out who it was that was coming to Asgard.

"In three half-years," declared the stranger, "I will build for you a castle so strong that not even the giants, should they swarm hither over Midgard – not even they could enter without your leave."

"Aha!" cried Father Odin, well pleased at this offer. "And what reward do you ask, friend, for help so timely?"

"I will name my price, friends," the stranger said, "a small price for so great a deed. I ask you to give me Freia for my wife, and those two sparkling jewels, the Sun and Moon."

At this demand the gods looked grave, for Freia was their dearest treasure. She was the most beautiful maid who ever lived, the light and life of heaven, and if she should leave Asgard, joy would go with her, while the Sun and Moon were the light and life of the gods' children, men, who lived in the little world below.

But Loki the sly whispered that they would be

safe enough if they made another condition on their part, so hard that the builder could not fulfil it. After thinking cautiously, he spoke for them all.

"Mighty man," quoth he, "we are willing to agree to your price – upon one condition. We cannot wait three half-years for our castle. See that you finish the fort without help in one winter – one short winter – and you shall have fair Freia with the Sun and Moon. But if, on the first day of summer, one stone is wanting to the walls, then you shall depart without payment."

At first the stranger shook his head and frowned, saying that in so short a time no one unaided could complete the undertaking. At last he made another offer. "Let me have but my good horse, Svadilföri, to help me with the task, and I will try," he urged. "Surely, you will not deny me this little help, from one four-footed friend."

Then again the gods consulted, but again Loki urged them to accept. "Surely, there is no harm," he said. "Even with an old horse to help them, no one could build the castle in the promised time. We shall gain a fortress without trouble and with never a price to pay."

Loki was so very eager that, although the other gods did not really agree with this crafty way of making bargains, they finally consented. Then the stranger and the gods gave solemn promise that the bargain should be kept.

On the first day of winter the strange builder began his work, and wondrous was the way he set about it. His strength seemed as the strength of a hundred men. As for his horse Svadilföri, he did more work by half than even the mighty builder. In the night he dragged the enormous rocks that were to be used in building the castle, rocks as big as mountains of the earth, while in the daytime the stranger piled them into place with his iron arms. The gods watched him with amazement, never was seen such strength in Asgard.

As the work went on, the gods began to look at one another uneasily. Who was this mighty one who had come among them, and what if after all he should win his reward? Freia trembled in her palace, and the Sun and Moon grew dim with fear.

Eventually the gods held a meeting upon Ida Plain, a meeting full of fear and anger. At last they realized what they had done – they had made a bargain with one of the giants, their enemies, and if he won the prize, it would mean sorrow and darkness in heaven and upon earth.

"It is your counsels, Loki, that have brought this danger upon us," said Father Odin, frowning. "If you cannot save Freia for us and the Sun and Moon, you shall die. This is my word." All the other gods agreed that this was just.

Loki was much frightened. "It was my fault, but how was I to know that he was a giant?" he cried. Then his face brightened. "Ha! I have a thought! The builder shall not finish the gate – the giant shall not receive his payment. I will cheat the fellow."

Now it was the last night of winter, and there

remained but a few stones to put in place on the top of the wondrous gateway. The giant was sure of his prize, and chuckled to himself as he went out with his horse to drag the remaining stones. However, hardly had he gone to work when out of the wood came running a pretty little mare, who neighed to Svadilföri as if inviting the tired horse to leave his work and come to the green fields for a holiday. Giving a snort of disobedience, off Svadilföri ran after this new friend towards the grassy meadows. Off went the giant after him, howling with rage, as he saw his chance of success slipping out of reach. It was a mad chase, and all Asgard thundered with the noise of galloping hoofs and the giant's mighty tread. The mare who raced ahead was Loki in disguise, and he led Svadilföri far out of reach, to a hidden meadow that he knew, so that the giant howled and panted up and down all night long, without catching even a sight of his horse.

Now when the morning came the gateway was

still unfinished, and night and winter had ended at the same hour. The giant's time was over, and he had forfeited his reward.

The delighted gods flocked to the gateway.

"You have failed, fellow," judged Father Odin sternly, "Leave Asgard quickly, we have seen all we want of you and of your race."

Then the giant knew that he was discovered, and he was mad with rage. "It was a trick!" he bellowed, assuming his own proper form, which was huge as a mountain, and towered high beside the fortress that he had built. "I will demolish your shining city!" Indeed, he would have done so in his mighty rage, but at this moment Thor, the mighty thunder god, came rushing to the rescue in his chariot of goats. Before the giant knew what had happened, his head was rolling upon the ground at Father Odin's feet, for with one blow Thor had saved Asgard.

In this extraordinary way the noble city of Asgard was made safe and complete by the addition of a fortress. But always at the top of the gate were lacking three great stones that no one was mighty enough to lift. This was a reminder to the gods that now they had the race of giants for their everlasting enemies. And though Loki's trick had saved them Freia, and for the world the Sun and Moon, it was the beginning of trouble in Asgard which lasted as long as Loki lived to make mischief with his guile.

Do You Believe in Fairies?

An extract from *Peter Pan* by J M Barrie

The home of the Darling children – Wendy, John and Michael – is often visited by a flying boy called Peter Pan. One night, Peter whisks the children to his home – Neverland – so Wendy can mother his gang, the Lost Boys. But Neverland is a dangerous place and, unfortunately, Wendy and her brothers are captured by Captain Hook and his evil band of pirates. Peter's best friend, a mischievous fairy called Tinker Bell, comes to break the bad news to him...

Peter slept on. The light guttered and went out, leaving the tenement in darkness, but still he slept. It must have been not less than ten o'clock, when he sat up in his bed, wakened by a soft, cautious tapping on the door of his tree.

Soft and cautious, but in that stillness it was
sinister. Peter felt for his dagger till his hand
gripped it. Then he spoke, "Who is that?"

For a long time there was no answer, but then
he heard the knock again.

"Who are you?"

No answer.

Peter was thrilled,
and he loved being
thrilled. In two
strides he reached
the door.

"I won't open unless
you speak," Peter cried.

Then at last the visitor
spoke, in a bell-like voice.

"Let me in, Peter."

It was Tink, and quickly he
unbarred to her. She flew in
excitedly, her face flushed and her
dress stained with mud.

"What is it?"

"Oh, you could never guess!" she cried, and offered him three guesses.

"Out with it!" he shouted, and in one ungrammatical sentence, as long as the ribbons that magicians pull from their mouths, she told of the capture of Wendy and the boys.

Peter's heart bobbed up and down as he listened. Wendy bound, and on the pirate ship – she who loved everything to be just so!

"I'll rescue her!" he cried, leaping at his weapons. As he leaped he thought of something he could do to please her. He could take his medicine.

His hand closed on the fatal draught.

"No!" shrieked Tinker Bell, who had heard Hook mutter about his deed as he sped through the forest.

"Why not?"

"It is poisoned."

"Poisoned? Who could have poisoned it?"

"Hook."

"Don't be silly. How indeed could Hook have got down here?"

Alas, Tinker Bell could not explain this. Nevertheless Hook's words had left no room for doubt. The cup was poisoned.

"Besides," said Peter, quite believing himself, "I never fell asleep."

He raised the cup. No time for words now, time for deeds, and with one of her lightning movements Tink got between his lips and the draught, and drained it to the dregs.

"Why, Tink, how dare you drink my medicine?"

But she did not answer. Already she was reeling in the air.

"What is the matter with you?" cried Peter, suddenly afraid.

"It was poisoned, Peter," she told him softly, "and now I am going to be dead."

"O Tink, did you drink it to save me?"

"Yes."

"But why, Tink?"

Her wings would scarcely carry her now, but in reply she alighted on his shoulder and gave his nose a loving bite. She whispered in his ear, "You silly ass," and then, tottering to her chamber, laid on the bed.

His head almost filled the fourth wall of her little room as he knelt near her in distress. Her light was growing fainter, and he knew that if it went out she would be no more. She liked his tears so much that she put out her finger and let them run over it.

Her voice was so low that at first he could not make out what she said. Then he made it out. She was saying that she thought she could get well again if

children believed in fairies.

There were no children there, and it was night time, but Peter addressed all who might be dreaming of the Neverland, and who were therefore near to him – boys and girls everywhere.

"Do you believe in fairies?" he cried.

Tink sat up in bed almost briskly to listen intently to her fate.

She fancied she heard answers in the affirmative, and then again she wasn't sure.

"What do you think?" she asked Peter.

"If you believe," he shouted to them, "clap your hands – don't let Tink die."

Many clapped.

Some didn't.

A few beastly ones hissed.

The clapping stopped suddenly, as if countless mothers had rushed to their children's bedrooms to see what on earth was happening, but already Tink was saved. Her voice grew strong, then she popped out of bed, then she was flashing through the room more merry and impudent than ever. She never thought of thanking those who believed, but she would have like to get at the ones who had hissed.

"And now to rescue Wendy!"

Arndt's Night Underground

From *Tales of Wonder Every Child Should Know*
by Kate Douglas Wiggin and Nora Archibald Smith

*I*t was on a dreary winter's night that two poor children were coming home from their work. Arndt and Reutha were tired, and as they came across the moor the wind blew in their faces.

"Dear Arndt, let me sit down and rest for a minute, I can go no farther," said Reutha, as she sank down on a little mound that seemed to rise up invitingly, with its shelter of bushes.

It was not a cold night, so Arndt wrapped his sister up in her woollen cloak, and she sat down.

"I will just run a little farther and try to see the

light in Father's window," said Arndt. "You will not be afraid, Reutha?"

"Oh, no! I am never afraid," said Reutha, and leaned her head against a mossy bank that seemed to her as soft and inviting as a pillow.

Arndt went a little way, until he saw the light that his father always placed to guide the children over the moor. Then he felt quite safe, and went back cheerfully to his sister.

Reutha was not there! Arndt searched beside the little mound and among the bushes in terror, but he could not find his sister. He called her name loudly – there was no answer. Not a single trace of her could be found, and yet he had not been five minutes away.

"Oh! What shall I do?" sobbed the boy, and sat for a long time by the hillock, wringing his hands in vain.

At last there passed by an old man, who travelled about the country selling ribbons and cloths. Arndt burst into tears and told him of all that had happened that night.

The peddler's face grew graver and graver. "Arndt," whispered he, "did you ever hear of the Hill-men? It is they who have carried little Reutha away." And then the old man told how in his youth he had heard tales of this same moor, for that the little mound was a fairy-hill, where the underground dwarfs lived, and where they often carried off young children to be their servants, taking them under the hill, and only leaving behind their shoes. "For," said the peddler, "the Hill-people are very particular, and will make all their servants wear beautiful glass shoes instead of clumsy leather."

So he and Arndt searched about the hill, and there, sure enough, they found Reutha's tiny shoes hidden under the long grass. At this her brother's tears burst forth afresh.

"Oh! What shall I do to bring back my poor sister? The Hill-men and women will kill her!"

"No," said the old man, "they will keep Reutha with them a hundred years, and when she comes back you will be dead and buried, while she is still a beautiful child." And then, to comfort the boy, the peddler told him wonderful stories of the riches and splendour of the Hill-people, how that sometimes they had been seen dancing at night on the mounds, and how they wore green caps, which, if any mortal man could get possession of, the dwarfs were obliged to serve him and obey him in everything.

All this Arndt drank in with eager ears, and when the peddler went away he sat a long time thinking.

"I will do it," at last he said aloud. "I will try to get my dear Reutha back safe again."

And the boy stole noiselessly to the mound where the Hill-men were supposed to dwell. He hid himself among the surrounding bushes, and there he lay in the silence and darkness. At last a sudden brightness flashed upon the boy's eyes, the grassy hill opened, and the boy saw a palace underground, glittering with gold and gems. The Hill-men danced about within it, dressed like tiny men and women. One by one they rose out of the opening, and gambolled on the snow-covered mound, but wherever they trod flowers sprang up, and the air grew light and warm as summer. After a while they ceased dancing and began ball-playing, tossing their little green caps about in great glee. And lo and behold! One of these wonderful caps, being tossed farther than usual, lighted on the very forehead of the peeping boy! In a moment he snatched it and held on to it fast, with a cry of triumph. The light faded – the scene vanished – only Arndt heard a small weak voice whispering, humbly and beseechingly in his ear.

"Please, noble gentleman, give me my cap again."

"No, no, good Hill-man," answered the boy, in a strong, courageous voice. "You have got my little sister, and I have got your cap, which I shall keep."

"I will give you a better cap for it – all gold and jewels – oh, so beautiful!" said the Hill-man, persuasively.

"I will not have it. What good would it do me? No, no, I am your master, good dwarf, as you very well know, and I command you to take me down in the hill with you, for I want to see Reutha."

Then Arndt saw the elfin mound open again, but this time the palace was at the bottom of what looked like a dim, gloomy staircase. On the top stair stood the little Hill-man, holding a glowworm lamp, and making many low bows to his new master. Arndt glanced rather fearfully down the staircase, but then he thought of Reutha, and his love for her made him grow bold. He took upon himself a lordly air, and bade his little servant lead the way.

The Hill-man took him through beautiful galleries, and halls, and gardens, until the boy's senses were overwhelmed with these lovely things. Every now and then he stopped, and asked for Reutha, but then there was always some new chamber to be seen, or some dainty banquet to be tasted, until, by degrees, Arndt's memory of his little sister grew dimmer. When night came, the boy felt himself lulled by sweet music to a soft

dreaminess, which was all the sleep that was needed in that fairy paradise.

Thus, day after day passed in all gay delights, the elfin people were the merriest in the world, and they did all their little master desired. And Arndt knew not that while they surrounded him with delights it was only to make him forget his errand.

But one day, when the boy lay on a green dell in the lovely fairy-garden, he heard a low, wailing song, and saw a troop of little mortal children at work in the distance. Some were digging ore, and others making jewellery, while a few stood in the stream that ran by, beating linen, as it seemed. And among these poor little maidens, who worked so hard and sang so mournfully, was his own sister Reutha.

"No one cares for me," she murmured, and her song had in it a plaintive sweetness, very different from the way in which the little maiden spoke on earth. "Poor Reutha is quite alone!"

Even amidst the spells of fairyland that voice went to the brother's heart. He called the Hill-people and bade them bring Reutha to him. Then he kissed her, and wept over her, and dressed her in his own beautiful robes, while the Hill-men dared not interfere. Arndt took his sister by the hand, and said, "Now, let us go – we have stayed here long enough. Good Hill-man, you shall have your cap again when you have brought Reutha and me to our own father's door."

But the Hill-man shook his tiny head, and made his most obsequious bow. "Noble master, anything but this! This little maid we found asleep on our hill, and she is ours for a hundred years."

Here Arndt got into a passion, for, convinced of the power the little green cap gave him over the dwarfs, he had long lost all fear of them. He stamped with his foot until the little man leaped up a yard high and begged and pleaded with his master to be more patient.

"How dare you keep my sister!" cried the boy, his former companion becoming at once hateful to him. And Arndt folded his arms around Reutha and walked with her through all the gorgeous rooms, the Hill-men and women following behind and luring him with their sweetest songs, most bewitching smiles and promises of great riches and treasures. But Reutha's voice and Reutha's smile had the greatest power of all over her brother's heart.

They climbed the gloomy staircase, and stood at the opening in the hillock. Arndt felt the breezes of earth playing on his cheek. How sweet they were, even after the fragrant airs of elfin-land!

"Kind master, give me my cap!" piteously implored the Hill-man.

"Take it, and goodbye for ever more!" cried Arndt, as he clasped his sister in his arms and leaped out. The chasm closed, and the two children found themselves lying in a snow-drift, with the grey dawn of a winter's morning just breaking over them.

"Where have you been all night, my children?" cried the anxious mother, as they knocked at the door.

Had it, indeed, been only a single night – the months that seemed to have passed while they were under the hill? They could not tell, for they were now like all other children, and their wisdom learned in fairyland had passed away. It seemed only a dream, save that the brother and sister loved each other better than ever, and so they continued to do as long as they lived.

Shipwreck on Lilliput

An extract from *Gulliver's Travels*
by Jonathan Swift, adapted by John Lang

*Lemuel Gulliver is a young surgeon who falls on hard times.
He takes work on board ships making long sea voyages to strange,
distant lands. On one such journey, far from home, a terrible storm
wrecks his ship, washing away all the crew and leaving Gulliver at
the mercy of the waves...*

Gulliver swam till no strength or feeling was left in his arms and legs. He swam bravely, his breath coming in sobs, his eyes blinded with the salty seas that broke over his head.

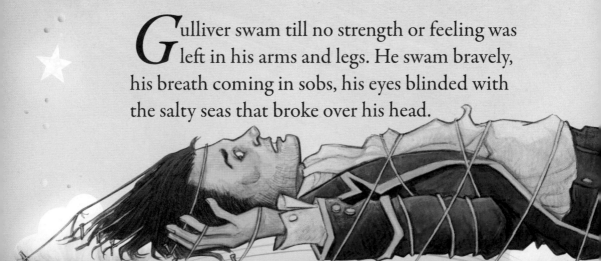

Still he struggled on, until at last, in a part where the wind seemed to have less force, on letting down his legs he found that he was within his depth. But the shore shelved so gradually that for nearly a mile he had to wade wearily through shallow water, till, almost fainting with fatigue, he reached dry land.

By this time darkness was coming on, and there were no signs of houses or of people. He staggered forward but a little distance, and then, on the short, soft turf, sank down exhausted and slept.

When he woke, the sun was shining. He tried to rise, but not by any means could he stir hand or foot. Gulliver had slept lying on his back, and now he found that his arms and legs were tightly fastened to the ground. Across his body were numbers of thin but strong cords, and even his hair, which was very long, was pegged down so securely that

he could not turn his head.

All round about him there was a confused sound of voices, but he could see nothing except the sky, and the sun shone so hot and fierce into his eyes that he could scarcely keep them open.

Soon he felt something come gently up his left leg, and forward on to his breast almost to his chin. Looking down as much as possible, he saw standing there a very little man, not more than six inches high, armed with a bow and arrows.

Then many more small men began to swarm over him. Gulliver let out such a roar of wonder and fright that they all turned and ran, many of them getting bad falls in their hurry to get out of danger. But very quickly the little people came back again. This time, with a great struggle Gulliver managed to break the cords that fastened his left arm, and at the same time, by a violent wrench that hurt him dreadfully, he slightly loosened the strings that fastened his hair, so that he was able to turn his head a little to one side. But the little men were too quick for him, and got out of reach before he could catch any of them.

Then he heard a great shouting, followed by a shrill little voice that called sharply, "Tolgo phonac," and immediately, arrows like needles were shot into his hand, and another volley struck him in the face. Poor Gulliver covered his face with his hand, and lay groaning with pain.

Again he struggled to get loose. But the harder he fought for freedom, the more the little men shot arrows into him, and some of them even tried to run their spears into his sides.

When he found that the more he struggled the more he was hurt, Gulliver lay still, thinking to himself that at night at least, now that his left hand was free, he could easily get rid of the rest of his bonds. As soon as the little people saw that he struggled no more, they ceased shooting at him, but he knew from the increasing sound of voices that more and more of the little soldiers were coming round him.

Soon, a few yards from him, on the right, he heard a continued sound of hammering, and on turning his head to that side as far as the strings would let him, he saw that a small wooden stage was being built. On to this, when it was finished, there climbed by ladders four men, and one of them (who seemed to be a very important person, for a little page boy attended to hold up his train) immediately gave an order. At once about fifty of the soldiers ran forward and cut the strings that tied Gulliver's hair on the left side, so that he could turn his head easily to the right.

Then the person began to make a long speech, not one word of which could Gulliver understand, but it seemed to him that sometimes the little man threatened and sometimes made offers of kindness.

As well as he could, Gulliver made signs that he submitted. Then, feeling by this time faint with hunger, he pointed with his fingers many times to his mouth, to show that he wanted something to eat.

They understood him very well. Several ladders were put against Gulliver's sides, and about a hundred little people climbed up and carried to his mouth all kinds of bread and meat. There were things shaped like legs, and shoulders, and saddles of mutton. Very good they were, Gulliver thought, but very small, no bigger than a lark's wing, and the loaves of bread were about the size of bullets, so that he could take several at a mouthful. The people wondered greatly at the amount that he ate.

When he signed that he was thirsty, they slung up two of their biggest casks of wine, and having rolled them forward to his hand they knocked out the heads of the casks. Gulliver drank them both and asked for more, for they held only about a small tumblerful each. But there was no more to be had.

As the small people walked to and fro over his

body, Gulliver was sorely tempted to seize forty or fifty of them and dash them on the ground, and then to make a further struggle for liberty. But the pain he had already suffered from their arrows made him think better of it, and he wisely lay quiet.

Soon another small man, who from his brilliant uniform seemed to be an officer of very high rank, marched with some others on to Gulliver's chest and held up to his eyes a paper that Gulliver understood to be an order from the king of the country. The officer made a long speech, often pointing towards something a long way off, and (as Gulliver afterwards learned) told him that he was to be taken as a prisoner to the city, the capital of the country.

The city was not reached till the following day, whereupon Gulliver was brought to a very large building that had once been used as a temple. Inside the building the king's blacksmiths fastened many chains, which they then brought through one of these little windows and padlocked round Gulliver's left ankle. Gulliver found that he could easily creep through the door, and that there was room inside to lie down. He could also get a little exercise by walking backwards and forwards outside. Then the king gave orders that food should be brought for Gulliver, twenty little carts full, and ten of wine, and he and his courtiers, all covered with gold and silver, stood around and watched him eating.

After the king had gone away, the people of the city crowded round, and some of them began to behave very badly, one man even going so far as to shoot an arrow at Gulliver which was not far from putting out one of his eyes. But the officer in command of the soldiers who were on guard ordered his men to bind and push six of the worst behaved of the crowd within reach of Gulliver, who at once seized five of them and put them in his coat pocket. The sixth he held up to his mouth and made as if he meant to eat him,

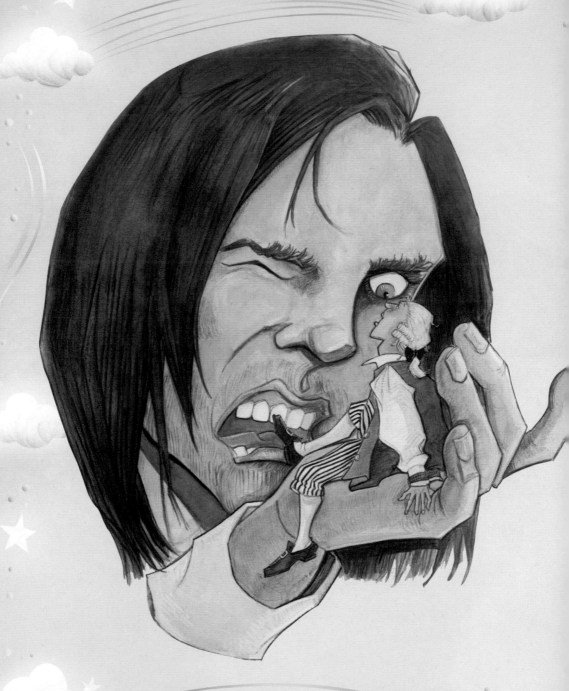

whereupon the wretched little creature shrieked aloud with terror, and when Gulliver took out his knife, all the people, even the soldiers, were dreadfully alarmed. But Gulliver only cut the man's bonds and let him run away, which he did in a great hurry. And when he took the others out of his pocket, one by one, and treated them in the same way, the crowd began to laugh.

After that the people always behaved very well to Gulliver, and he became a great favourite. From all over the kingdom crowds flocked to see the Great Man Mountain.

A Grin Without a Cat

An extract from *Alice's Adventures in Wonderland*
by Lewis Carroll

Alice follows a talking, clothed White Rabbit down a rabbit hole and falls into a dreamlike place where anything can happen. She drinks a drink that shrinks her and eats a cake which makes her grow. She weeps a sea of tears and talks to animals and birds who are washed away. A caterpillar helps her return to her proper size, whereupon she meets a Duchess whose baby turns into a pig and runs away. Then, high in a nearby tree, a strange cat appears...

The cat only grinned when it saw Alice. It looked good-natured, she thought. Still it had VERY long claws and a great many teeth, so she felt that it ought to be treated with respect.

"Cheshire Puss," she began, rather timidly, as

she did not at all know whether it would like the name, however, it only grinned a little wider. 'Come, it's pleased so far,' thought Alice, and she went on. "Would you tell me, please, which way I ought to go from here?"

"That depends a good deal on where you want to get to," said the Cat.

"I don't much care where—" said Alice.

"Then it doesn't matter which way you go," said the Cat.

"—so long as I get SOMEWHERE," Alice added as an explanation.

"Oh, you're sure to do that," said the Cat, "if you only walk long enough."

Alice felt that this could not be denied, so she tried another question. "What sort of people live about here?"

"In THAT direction," the Cat said, waving its right paw round, "lives a Hatter, and in THAT direction," waving the other paw, "lives a March Hare. Visit either you like – they're both mad."

"But I don't want to go among mad people," Alice remarked.

"Oh, you can't help that," said the Cat, "we're all mad here. I'm mad. You're mad."

"How do you know I'm mad?" said Alice.

"You must be," said the Cat, "or you wouldn't have come here."

Alice didn't think that this proved it at all, however, she went on, "And how do you know that you're mad?"

"To begin with," said the Cat, "a dog's not mad. You grant that?"

"I suppose so," said Alice.

"Well, then," the Cat went on, "you see, a dog growls when it's angry, and wags its tail when it's pleased. Now I growl when I'm pleased, and wag my tail when I'm angry. Therefore I'm mad."

"I call it purring, not growling," said Alice.

"Call it what you like," said the Cat. "Do you play croquet with the queen today?"

"I should like it very much," said Alice, "but I

haven't been invited yet."

"You'll see me there," said the Cat, and vanished.

Alice was not much surprised at this, she was getting so used to queer things happening. While she was looking at the place where it had been, it suddenly appeared again.

"By-the-bye, what became of the baby?" said the Cat. "I'd nearly forgotten to ask."

"It turned into a pig," Alice quietly said, just as if it had come back in a natural way.

"I thought it would," said the Cat, and vanished again.

Alice waited a little, half expecting to see it again, but it did not appear, and after a minute or two she walked on in the direction in which the March Hare was said to live. "I've seen hatters before," she said to herself, "the March Hare will be much the most interesting, and perhaps as this is May it won't be raving mad – at least not so mad as it was in March." As she said this, she looked up, and there was the Cat again, sitting on a branch of a tree.

"Did you say pig, or fig?" said the Cat.

"I said pig," replied Alice, "and I do wish that you wouldn't keep appearing and vanishing so very suddenly – you make one quite giddy."

"All right," said the Cat, and this time it vanished quite slowly, beginning with the end of the tail, and ending with the grin, which remained some time after the rest of it had gone.

'Well! I've often seen a cat without a grin,' thought Alice, 'but a grin without a cat! It's the most curious thing I ever saw in my life!'

The Deliverers of their Country

An extract from the tale in *The Book of Dragons*
by E Nesbit

There was no one about in the streets except dragons, and the place was swarming with them. Fortunately none were just the right size for eating little boys and girls. There were dragons on the pavement, and dragons on the roadway, dragons basking on the front doorsteps of public buildings, and dragons preening their wings on the roofs in the hot afternoon sun. The town was quite green with them. Even when the children had got out of the town and were walking in the lanes, they noticed that the fields on each side were greener than usual with the scaly legs and tails, and some of the smaller sizes had made themselves asbestos nests in the flowering hawthorn hedges.

Effie held her brother's hand tight, and when a fat dragon flopped against her ear she screamed, and a whole flight of dragons rose from the field at the sound, and sprawled away across the sky.

"Oh, I want to go home," said Effie.

"No," said Harry. "People who are going to be their country's deliverers don't say they want to go home."

"Are we?" asked Effie, "Deliverers, I mean?"

"You'll see," said her brother, and they carried on.

When they came to St George's Church they walked around the churchyard, and presently found the

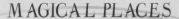

large stone tomb, with the figure of St George carved in marble, wearing his armour and helmet, and with his hands folded across his breast.

"However can we wake him?" they said. Then Harry spoke to St George and tried to waken the great dragon-slayer by shaking his marble shoulders. But St George took no notice.

Then Effie began to cry, and she put her arms around St George's neck and she kissed the marble face, and she said, "Oh, dear, good, kind St George, please wake up and help us."

And at that St George opened his eyes sleepily, and stretched himself and said, "What's the matter, little girl?"

So the children told him all about it, but when he heard that there were so many dragons he shook his head.

"It's no good," he said. 'One man one dragon' was my motto."

At that moment a flight of dragons passed overhead and

St George half drew his sword.

"By the way, what sort of weather have you been having lately?"

Effie said patiently, "It has been very fine. Father says it is the hottest weather there has ever been in this country."

"Ah, I guessed as much," said the champion, thoughtfully. "Dragons can't stand wet and cold. If only you could find the taps…"

St George was beginning to settle down again on his stone slab.

"Goodnight, very sorry I can't help you," he said, yawning behind his marble hand.

"Oh," cried Effie. "What taps do you mean?"

"Oh, like in the bathroom," said St George, still more sleepily. "I'm sorry I can't – goodnight."

And he fell back into his marble and was fast asleep again in a moment.

The Enchanted Horse 250

The Princess on the Glass Hill 261

The Storks and the Night Owl 274

The Feast of the Lanterns 288

ENCHANTMENTS AND TRANSFORMATIONS

The Old Man and the Gift 300

The Well of the World's End 307

The Crystal Coffin 313

The Enchanted Horse

From *The Arabian Nights Entertainments*,
adapted by Amy Steedman

*I*t was New Year's day in Persia, and the king had been entertained by many wonderful shows prepared by his people. Evening was drawing on when an Indian appeared, leading a horse he wished to show to the king. It was not real, but it was so wonderfully made that it looked alive.

"Your Majesty," cried the Indian, bowing low, "I beg you to look at this wonder. Nothing you have seen can equal my horse. I have only to sit on its back and wish myself in any part of the

world, and it carries me there in a few minutes."

"Show us what it can do," the king commanded. He pointed to a distant mountain, and bade the Indian to fetch a branch from the palm trees there.

The Indian vaulted into the saddle, turned a little peg in the horse's neck, and in a moment was flying so swiftly through the air that he soon disappeared from sight. In less than a quarter of an hour he reappeared, and laid a branch from a palm tree at the king's feet.

"Yes," cried the king. "Your enchanted horse is the most wonderful thing I have seen. What is its price? I must have it!"

"Your Majesty," the Indian replied, "it shall be yours if you will let me marry your daughter."

At these words the king's son sprang to his feet.

"Sire," he cried, "you would never dream of granting such a request."

"Son," said the king, "at whatever cost I must have this wonderful horse. But before I agree, try the horse, and tell me what you think of it."

The Indian began to tell the prince how to work the horse. But as soon as the prince was in the saddle, he turned the screw and went flying off through the air.

"Alas!" cried the Indian, "he has gone before learning how to return!"

"Wretch," the king cried, "you shall be cast into prison, and unless my son returns in safety, you will be put to death."

Meanwhile the prince had gone gaily sailing up into the clouds, and could no longer see the Earth below. This was very pleasant, and he felt that he had never had such a delicious ride in his life before. But presently he began to think it was time to descend. He screwed the peg round and

round, backwards and
forwards, but it seemed to
make no difference. Instead
of coming down he sailed
higher, until he thought he
was going to knock his head
against the blue sky.

What was to be done? The
prince began to grow a little
nervous, and he felt over the horse's
neck to see if there was another peg to be found
anywhere. To his joy, just behind the ear, he
touched a small screw, and when he turned it, he
felt he was going slower and slower, and gently
turning round. Then the Enchanted Horse flew
downwards through the starry night, and the
prince saw, stretched out before him, a beautiful
city gleaming white through the purple night.

He let the horse go where it would, and
presently it stopped on the roof of a great marble
palace. He descended some white marble steps

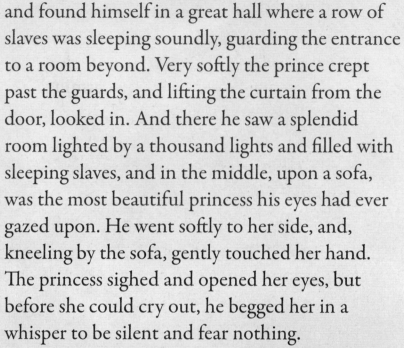

and found himself in a great hall where a row of
slaves was sleeping soundly, guarding the entrance
to a room beyond. Very softly the prince crept
past the guards, and lifting the curtain from the
door, looked in. And there he saw a splendid
room lighted by a thousand lights and filled with
sleeping slaves, and in the middle, upon a sofa,
was the most beautiful princess his eyes had ever
gazed upon. He went softly to her side, and,
kneeling by the sofa, gently touched her hand.
The princess sighed and opened her eyes, but
before she could cry out, he begged her in a
whisper to be silent and fear nothing.

"I am the son of the King of Persia."

Now this princess was no other than the
daughter of the King of Bengal.

Never before had the princess seen anyone so
gallant and handsome as this strange young
prince. She gave him her hand, awoke her slaves
and bade them give him refreshment. While the
prince rested, she dressed herself in her loveliest

robes, and twined her hair with her most precious jewels, that she might appear as beautiful as possible. And when the prince saw her again, he thought her the most charming princess in all the world, and he loved her with all his heart. When he had told her all his adventures she sighed to think that he must now leave her and return to his father's court.

"My princess," he said, "since it is so hard to part, will you not ride with me upon the Enchanted Horse? Then when we arrive once more in Persia we will marry."

So together they mounted the Enchanted Horse and the prince placed his arm around the princess and turned the magic peg. Up and up they flew over land and sea, and then the prince turned the other screw, and they landed just outside his father's city. He left the princess at a palace outside the gates, for he wished to go alone to prepare his father.

"My Son!" cried the king, joyful at his return.

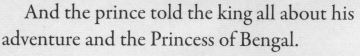

And the prince told the king all about his adventure and the Princess of Bengal.

"Let her be brought here," cried the king, "and the marriage shall take place today." Then he ordered that the Indian should be set free and allowed to depart with the Enchanted Horse.

Great was the surprise of the Indian when he was released instead of having his head cut off, as he had expected. But when he heard about the prince's adventure, a wicked plan came into his head. He flew on the Enchanted Horse to the palace where the princess was waiting, arriving before the king's messengers could reach her. "Tell the princess," he said to the palace slaves, "that the Prince of Persia has sent me to bring her to his father's palace upon the Enchanted Horse."

The princess was very glad when she heard this message – but alas! As soon as the Indian turned the peg and the horse flew away, she found she was being carried off, far away from Persia and her beloved prince. All her prayers and entreaties

were in vain. The Indian only mocked her and said he meant to marry her himself.

When the prince discovered what had happened, he was beside himself with grief. He set off to look for her, vowing that he would find her, or perish in the attempt.

By this time the Enchanted Horse had travelled many hundreds of miles. The Indian descended into a wood close to the town of Cashmere, where he went in search of food. As soon as the princess had eaten a little she felt stronger and braver, and as she heard horses galloping past, she called out loudly for help. The men on horseback came riding at once to her aid. The leader of the horsemen, who was the Sultan of Cashmere, cut off the Indian's head, placed the princess upon his horse and led her to his palace. He had made up his mind to marry her himself!

In vain the princess begged and pleaded to be sent back to Persia. But the sultan only smiled and began the wedding preparations. Then she

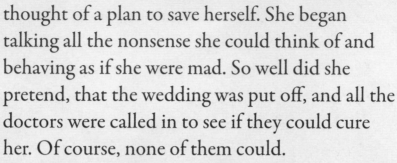

thought of a plan to save herself. She began talking all the nonsense she could think of and behaving as if she were mad. So well did she pretend, that the wedding was put off, and all the doctors were called in to see if they could cure her. Of course, none of them could.

All this time the Prince of Persia was searching for his princess, and when he came to one of the great cities of India, he quickly learned that everyone was talking about the sad illness of the Princess of Bengal who was to marry the sultan. He at once disguised himself as a doctor and went to the palace. The sultan received him with joy, and led him at once to where the princess sat alone, weeping and wringing her hands.

"Your Majesty," said the disguised prince, "no one must enter the room with me, or the cure will surely fail and the princess will never recover."

So the sultan left him, and the prince went to the princess, and touched her hand. "My beloved princess," he said, "do you not know me?"

As soon as the princess heard that dear voice she threw herself into the prince's arms.

"We must at once plan our escape," said the prince. "Can you tell me what has become of the Enchanted Horse?"

"Nothing can I tell you of it, dear prince," said the princess, "but since the sultan knows its value, no doubt he has kept it in some safe place."

"Then first we must persuade the sultan that you are almost cured," said the prince. "Put on your most expensive robes and dine with him tonight, and I will do the rest."

The sultan was charmed to find the princess so much recovered, and his joy knew no bounds when the new doctor informed him that he hoped by the next day to have the cure complete.

"I find that the princess has somehow been infected by the magic of the Enchanted Horse," he said. "If you will have the horse brought out into the great square, and place the princess upon its back, I will prepare some magic perfumes that will dispel the enchantment."

So the next morning the Enchanted Horse was brought into the square, which was crowded with onlookers, and the princess was mounted upon its back. Then the disguised prince placed four braziers of burning coals round the horse and threw into them a delicious perfume. The smoke of the perfume rose in thick clouds, almost hiding the princess, and at that moment the prince leaped into the saddle behind her, turned the peg, and sailed away into the blue sky.

The Enchanted Horse did not stop until it had carried the two of them safely back to Persia, and there they were married amid great rejoicings.

But what became of the Enchanted Horse? Ah! That is a question that no one can answer.

The Princess on the Glass Hill

From Andrew Lang's *Blue Fairy Book*

Once upon a time there was a man who had a meadow that lay on a mountain, and in the meadow there was a barn in which he stored hay. But there had not been much hay for the last two years, for every St John's eve, when the grass was highest, it was all eaten clean up, as if a whole flock of sheep had gnawed it during the night. The man became tired of losing his crop, and said to his sons – he had three, and the third was called Cinderlad – that one of them must sleep in the barn on St John's night and keep a look-out,

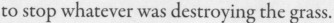

to stop whatever was destroying the grass.

The eldest was quite willing to go to the meadow. He would watch so well, he said, that neither man, nor beast, nor even the Devil himself should have any of it. So when evening came he went to the barn and lay down to sleep, but when night was drawing on there was such a rumbling and earthquake that the walls and roof shook. The lad took to his heels as fast as he could, never even looking back, so the barn remained empty that year too.

Next St John's eve, the next eldest son was willing to show what he could do. He went to the barn and lay down to sleep, as his brother had done. But when night was drawing near there was a great rumbling, and then an earthquake even worse than that on the former St John's night. When the terrified youth heard it he ran off.

The year after, it was Cinderlad's turn, but when he prepared to go, the others mocked him. "Well, you are just the right one to watch the hay,

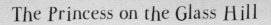

you who have never learned anything but how to sit among the ashes!" said they.

Cinderlad, however, did not trouble himself about what they said, but when evening drew near rambled away to the outlying field. When he got there he went into the barn and lay down, but in about an hour's time the rumbling and creaking began, and it was frightful to hear it.

'Well, if it gets no worse than that, I can manage to stand it,' thought Cinderlad. In a little time the creaking began again, and the earth quaked so that all the hay flew about.

'Oh! If it gets no worse than that I can manage to stand it,' thought Cinderlad. But then came a third rumbling, and a third earthquake, so violent that the boy thought the walls and roof had fallen down, but when that was over everything suddenly grew as still.

'I am pretty sure that it will come again,' thought Cinderlad, but no, it did not. Everything was quiet, and everything stayed quiet, and when he had lain still a short time he heard something that sounded as if a horse were standing chewing just outside the barn door.

He stole away to the door, which was ajar, to see what was there, and a horse was standing eating. It was so big, and fat, and fine a horse that Cinderlad had never seen one like it before, and a saddle and bridle lay upon it, and a complete suit of armour for a knight, and everything was of copper, and shone brightly.

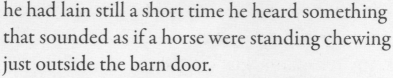

'Ha, ha! It is you who eatst up our hay then,' thought the boy. 'I will stop that'.

He made haste, and took out his steel for striking fire, and threw it over the horse, and then

it had no power to stir from the spot, and became so tame that the boy could do what he liked with it. So he mounted it and rode to a place that no one knew of but himself, and there he tied it up.

When he went home again his brothers sniggered and asked how he had got on.

"I lay in the barn till the sun rose, but I saw and heard nothing," said the boy. "God knows what there was to make you two so frightened."

And when the puzzled brothers went to check the meadow, the grass was all standing just as long and as thick as it had been the night before.

The next St John's eve, Cinderlad went again, and three earthquakes happened exactly as before. This time the horse that arrived was far larger and fatter than the first horse, and it had a saddle on its back, and a bridle was on it too, and a full suit of armour for a knight, all of bright silver, and as beautiful as anyone could wish to see. Again the boy took out his steel for striking fire, and threw it over the horse's mane, and the beast stood there as quiet as a lamb. Then the boy rode the horse away to where he kept the other, and then went home again.

Once more, in the morning, the astounded brothers found the meadow grass standing as high and as thick as ever, but that did not make them any kinder to Cinderlad.

When the third St John's night came, once more Cinderlad dared to go, and everything happened just the same. There were three earthquakes, each worse than the last, and then there was a horse standing outside the barn, much larger and fatter than the two others he had caught. Again the boy pulled out his steel for striking fire, and threw it over the horse, and the boy could do just what he liked with it. He mounted it and rode to the place where he had the two others, and then he went home again.

The brothers hated him, for again the grass was standing, looking as fine and as thick as ever.

Now the king of the country had a palace close

to a high hill of glass, as slippery as ice. One day,
the king sent out a proclamation saying that he
would give his daughter's hand in marriage – and
half the kingdom – to any man who could ride to
the top of the glass hill, where his daughter was to
sit, and take one of three gold apples she would
hold in her lap.

On the appointed day, princes and knights
came riding thither from the very end of the
world to win the beautiful princess, and everyone
else thronged to the glass hill to see who won her.
Cinderlad's two brothers went along too, but
they would not hear of letting him go with them,
for he was so dirty with sleeping among the ashes
that they said everyone would laugh at them if
they were seen in the company of such an oaf.

"Well, then, I will go all alone," said Cinderlad.

When the two brothers got to the glass hill,
princes and knights were trying to ride up it –
but no sooner did the horses set foot upon the
hill then down they slipped, and not one could

get even so much as a couple of yards up.

At last all the horses were so tired that they could do no more, and their riders were forced to give up. Suddenly a knight in copper armour came riding up on a horse with copper bridle and saddle, shining like the dawn. He rode straight to the hill and began going up as if it were nothing at all. The princess thought that she had never seen so handsome a knight, and hoped that he might make it to the top. But when the knight had got about a third of the way up, he suddenly turned his horse round and rode down again. The disappointed princess threw one of the golden apples down after him, and it rolled into his shoe. But when he had come down from the hill he rode off so fast that no one knew what had become of him.

That night, Cinderlad's brothers returned with the story of the copper

knight and his horse riding up the glass hill.

"I should have liked to have seen him too," said Cinderlad as he sat in the cinders.

The next day the brothers set out again, and once more refused to let Cinderlad go with them. All the princes and knights were beginning to ride again, and this time they had taken care to roughen the their horses shoes – but that did not help them. They rode and they slipped as they had done the day before,

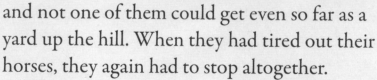

and not one of them could get even so far as a
yard up the hill. When they had tired out their
horses, they again had to stop altogether.

But all at once a knight in silver armour came
riding on a steed that was much, much finer than
the horse in copper tack. This one had a silver
bridle and saddle, and he and his rider shone like
the moon. He rode straight to the glass hill and
began to go up. The princess liked this knight
even better than she had liked the other, and sat
longing that he might be able to get all the way
up. But when the knight had ridden two-thirds
of the way up he suddenly turned his horse
around and rode down again. The dismayed
princess threw an apple after him, and it rolled
into his shoe, and as soon as he had got down the
glass hill he rode away so fast that no one could
see what had become of him.

At night the two brothers went home full of
news of the knight in silver armour.

"Oh, how I should have liked to have seen him

too!" said Cinderlad, from the dirty woodpile.

On the third day everything went just as on the former days. Cinderlad wanted to go with them to look at the riding, but the two brothers would not have him, and when they got to the glass hill there was no one who could ride even so far as a yard up it. Then there came thundering a knight in golden armour, riding a stallion without equal, wearing a golden saddle and bridle, and they blazed like the noonday sun. The knight rode straight away to the glass hill, and galloped up it as if it were no hill at all, so that the princess had not even time to wish that he might get up the whole way before he was at the top. The golden knight took the third golden apple from the lap of the princess and then turned his horse about and rode down again, and vanished from sight before anyone was able to say a word to him.

When the brothers returned home, they told Cinderlad of the knight in the golden armour.

"Oh, if only I could have seen him!" said Cinderlad, scrubbing the scullery floor.

Next day all the knights and princes were to appear before the king and princess, in order that he who had the golden apple might produce it. One after the other they all came, but no one had the golden apple. First princes, then knights went... then all the other young men of the kingdom. Cinderlad's two brothers were the last of all, and the king enquired of them if there was no one else left to come.

"We have a brother," said the two, "but he never got the golden apple! He never left the kitchen on any of the three days."

"Never mind that," said the king. "As everyone else has come to the palace, let him come too."

So Cinderlad went to the king's palace.

"Do you have the golden apple?" asked the king.

"Yes, here is the first, and here is the second, and here is the third, too," said Cinderlad, and he

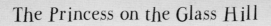

took all three apples out of his pocket, and with that removed his sooty rags, and appeared before them in his bright golden armour, which gleamed as he stood there.

"You shall have my daughter, and the half of my kingdom, and you have well earned both!" said the king. So there was a wedding, and Cinderlad got the king's daughter, and everyone made merry at the wedding, for all of them could make merry, even though they could not ride up the glass hill. And if they have not stopped their merry-making they must be at it still.

The Storks and the Night Owl

From *Tales of Wonder Every Child Should Know*
by Kate Douglas Wiggin and Nora Archibald Smith

*C*hasid, the Caliph of Baghdad, was comfortably seated upon his sofa one beautiful afternoon. He smoked from a long pipe made of rosewood, sipped now and then a little coffee, which a slave poured out for him, and stroked his beard very contentedly. So it was very plain that the caliph was in a good humour.

Just then, his grand vizier, Manzor, brought in a merchant with a chest that contained very interesting wares: pearls and rings, richly inlaid pistols, goblets and combs. The caliph and his

vizier looked at them and purchased some trinkets. As the merchant was about to pack up his chest the caliph noticed a small, strange box. On opening it, he found it was filled with blackish powder and a paper with strange writing upon it, which neither the caliph nor Manzor could read. "I received these things from a trader who found them in the streets of Mecca," explained the merchant. "I know not what they contain. They are at your service for a trifling price, for I can do nothing with them."

The caliph, who was a great collector of old manuscripts for his library, even if he could not read them, purchased box and writings, and dismissed the merchant. Then, in the hope of finding out what the writings meant, he sent for a man called Selim the Wise.

For a long time Selim examined the writing, before pronouncing the translation. "Oh man, thou who findest this, praise Allah for His great goodness to thee. Whoever snuffs of the powder

contained in this box, and says thereupon
'Mutabor', will have the power to change himself
into any animal he may choose, and will be able
to understand the language of that animal and all
others. Should he wish to return to his human
form he must bow himself three times to the
East, and in the direction of our holy Mecca, and
repeat the same word. But beware, when thou art
transformed that thou laughest not, otherwise
the magic word will disappear completely from
thy memory and thou wilt remain a beast."

The caliph was delighted beyond measure. He
made Selim vow that he would not disclose the
secret to anyone, and dismissed him. Then he
commanded the grand vizier to return early next
morning, when they would go out into the fields
and try out the magic.

The next day, not long after dawn, the caliph
and his grand vizier went through the gardens of
the caliph to a quiet pond, where they would be
alone. When they arrived they saw a stork

walking gravely up and down looking for frogs, and now and then clacking something to himself. Far above in the air, another stork hovered.

"I am pretty sure," said the grand vizier, "that these two long-legged fellows are carrying on a fine conversation with each other. What if we should become storks?"

"Well said!" replied the caliph. "But first let us consider, once more, how we are to become men again. True! Three times must we bend towards the East and in the direction of Mecca, and say 'Mutabor', then I am caliph again and you vizier. But we must take care whatever we do, not to laugh, or we are lost."

While the caliph was thus speaking he saw the other stork hover over their heads and slowly descend towards the earth. He drew the box quickly from his girdle, took a good pinch, offered it to the grand vizier, who also snuffed it, and both cried out, "Mutabor!"

At once their legs began to shrivel up, and

soon became thin and red. The beautiful yellow slippers of the caliph and his companion were changed into the strange-shaped feet of the stork, while their arms became wings, and their necks were lengthened from their shoulders and became a yard long. Their bodies were covered with feathers that were soft, fine and graceful, and their beards disappeared, and their faces changed, one after the other.

"You have a very beautiful beak," said the caliph after a long pause of astonishment.

"I thank you most humbly," replied the grand vizier, while he made his obeisance. "And I must say that Your Highness looks even more handsome as a stork than as a caliph. But come, if it please you, let us listen to our comrades yonder, and find out whether we really understand the language of the storks."

In the meantime the other stork had reached the ground. He trimmed his feet with his beak, put his feathers in order, and advanced towards his companion. The two new storks hastened to get near them, and to their surprise they heard the following conversation:

"Good morning, Lady Longlegs, already so early in the meadow."

"Thank you, dear Clatterbeak, I have had only a slight breakfast."

"Would you like, perhaps, a piece of a duck or the leg of a frog?"

"Much obliged, but I have no appetite. I have come to the meadow for a very different purpose. I am to dance today before guests of my father's, and I wish to practise here quietly by myself."

The young stork immediately jumped about the field with singular motions. The caliph and Manzor looked on with wonder, but as she stood in a picturesque attitude upon one foot, and fluttered her wings gracefully, they could no longer contain themselves – an irresistible laughter burst forth from their beaks, from which they could not recover themselves for a long time.

Suddenly it occurred to the grand vizier that laughter had been specially forbidden them during their transformation. He told his anxiety to the caliph. "Dear me, dear me, it would indeed be a sorrowful joke if I must remain a stork. Pray think of the magic word. For the life of me I can't remember it."

"Three times must we bow to the East and to Mecca, and then say, 'Mu, mu, mu.'"

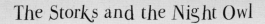

They turned towards the East, and bowed and bowed, so that their beaks almost touched the earth. But alas! The magic word would not come. All recollection of it had vanished, and the poor caliph and vizier remained storks.

They knew not what to do in their great distress. Very mournfully, they wandered about, eating only fruit, for they had no appetite for ducks and frogs. Then they flew upon the roofs of Baghdad to see what passed in the city.

During the first days they observed great mourning in the streets, but on the fourth day, they saw a splendid procession. Drums and flutes sounded, and a man in a scarlet mantle, embroidered with gold, rode a fine steed, surrounded by a brilliant train of attendants.

Half Baghdad leaped to meet him, and all cried, "Hail, Mirza, Lord of Baghdad!" The two storks looked at each other, and the caliph said, "All this must have been a plot – and we fell for it! This Mirza is the son of my deadly enemy, the

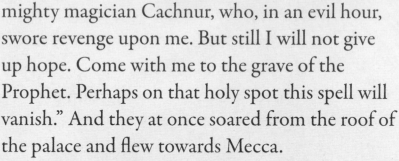

mighty magician Cachnur, who, in an evil hour, swore revenge upon me. But still I will not give up hope. Come with me to the grave of the Prophet. Perhaps on that holy spot this spell will vanish." And they at once soared from the roof of the palace and flew towards Mecca.

They flew until evening began to draw in, then looked for a place to shelter for the night. Seeing a ruin in the valley below, they swooped down and found themselves in what was formerly a castle. The storks wandered through crumbling passages and halls to find a dry spot for themselves. Suddenly the stork Manzor stopped. "My lord and master," he whispered, "I am sure that something nearby us sighed and groaned."

The caliph also stood still, and heard very distinctly a low weeping. Bravely, he hastened through a dark passageway and into a ruined chamber. It was dimly lit by a small grated window, and he saw a night owl upon the floor. Big tears rolled from her large round eyes, and

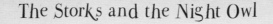

with a hoarse voice she sent forth her cries from her curved beak. As soon, however, as she saw the caliph and vizier she gave a loud scream of joy. Gracefully she wiped the tears from her eyes with her brown-spotted wing, and to the great astonishment of both she exclaimed, "Welcome, storks! You are a good sign of my rescue, for it has been told to me that by a stork I shall attain to great happiness."

When the caliph had recovered from his astonishment he related his own story, and the owl told the two storks hers. "My father is King of India. I, his only daughter, am called Lusa. That magician Cachnur, who has enchanted you, has also plunged me into this misery," she said.

"There must be a secret connection between our fates," pondered the caliph. "But where can I find the key to this riddle?"

The owl replied, "The magician comes once in every month to these ruins. Not far from this chamber is a hall. There he is accustomed to feast with many of his companions. I have often listened there. They tell one another their histories, and what they have been doing since last they met. Perhaps on the next occasion they may talk over your story, and let fall the magic word that you have forgotten."

"Dearest princess," exclaimed the caliph, "tell me when does he come and where is the hall?"

The owl was silent for a moment and then spoke. "I will tell you on one condition."

"Speak out!" cried the caliph. "Command, and whatever it is, I will obey."

"It is this: I also would gladly be free of my enchantment, and this can only happen if one of you offer me his hand in marriage."

The caliph agreed at once. Of course, the owl was overjoyed, and she said they could not have come at a better time, for the magicians would

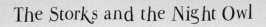

most likely meet that night. She then led them to
the hall entrance, advising them to keep perfectly
quiet. From the opening near where they stood
they had a good view. The hall had many pillars,
and was richly decorated. In the middle was a
round table covered with a feast, and around the
table sat eight men. The storks recognized one
man as the merchant who had sold them the
magic powder! The one who sat next to him
asked him to tell his history and what had been
done during the last few days. He did so, and
among the other things he told the story of his
visit to the caliph and grand vizier of Baghdad.

"What kind of a word have you given them?"
asked the other magician.

"A very hard Latin one – it is 'Mutabor'."

As the storks heard this from their place of
concealment they became almost beside
themselves for joy. They ran so quickly with their
long legs to the door of the ruin that the owl
could scarcely follow them. There, the caliph

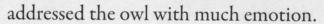
addressed the owl with much emotion.

"Saviour of my life, and the life of my friend, as an eternal thanks for what you have done for us, accept me as thy husband," then he turned himself towards the east and towards Mecca. Three times the storks bent their long necks towards the sun, which, by this time, was rising above the distant hills. "Mutabor!" they exclaimed. In a twinkling they were changed, and in the delight of newly restored life, master and servant were laughing and weeping in each other's arms. But who can describe their astonishment as they looked about them?

A beautiful maiden in a splendid dress stood before them. She held out her hand to the caliph saying, "Do you not recognize your night owl?"

The caliph looked with wonder at her beauty and grace, and said, "It is my greatest happiness that I have been a stork."

The three travelled together to Baghdad, where the caliph's people – who had supposed

him dead – were overjoyed to have their beloved lord again. And long and happily the caliph lived with his wife, the princess, with many pleasant hours when the grand vizier visited him in the afternoon. They never tired of talking about their storks' adventure, and when the caliph was more than usually merry he would imitate the grand vizier, and show how he looked when he was a stork. He walked gravely up and down the chamber with slow and solemn steps, made a clacking noise, flapped his arms like wings, and showed how he, to no purpose, bowed himself to the east and called out, "Mu—Mu—Mu." This was always a great delight to the princess and the children, which were afterwards born to her, until they also took delight in calling out to one another, "Mu—Mu—Mu."

The Feast of the Lanterns

From *Tales of Wonder Every Child Should Know*
by Kate Douglas Wiggin and Nora Archibald Smith

*W*ang Chih was only a poor man, but he had a wife and children to love, and they made him so happy that he would not have changed places with the emperor himself.

One morning, as he was setting off to work in the fields, his wife sent Han Chung, his son, after him to ask him to bring home some firewood.

"I shall have to go up into the mountain for it at noon," he said. "Bring me my axe, Han Chung."

Han Chung ran back for his father's axe, and Ho-Seen-Ko, his little sister, came out of the

cottage with him.

"Remember it is the Feast of Lanterns tonight, Father," she said. "Don't fall asleep up on the mountain, we want you to come back and light them for us."

She had a lantern in the shape of a fish, painted red and black and yellow, and Han Chung had a big round one, all bright crimson, to carry in the procession, and, besides that, there were two large lanterns to be hung outside the cottage door as soon at it grew dark.

Wang Chih was not likely to forget the Feast of Lanterns, for the children had talked of nothing else for a month, and he promised to come home as early as he could.

At noon, when his fellow-labourers sat down to rest and eat, Wang Chih took his axe and went up the mountain to find a small tree he might cut down for fuel. He walked a long way, and at last saw one growing at the mouth of a cave. "This will be just the thing," he said to himself. Before

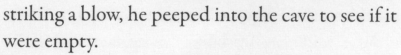

striking a blow, he peeped into the cave to see if it were empty.

To his surprise, two old men, with long, white beards, were sitting inside playing chess, as quietly as mice, with their eyes fixed on the chessboard. Wang Chih knew something of chess, and he stepped in and watched them for a few minutes. "As soon as they look up I can ask them if I may chop down a tree," he said to himself. But they did not look up, and by and by Wang Chih got so interested in the game that he put down his axe, and sat on the floor to watch it better.

The two old men sat crosslegged on the ground, and the chessboard rested on a slab, like a stone table, between them. On one corner of the slab lay a heap of small, brown objects which Wang Chih took at first to be date stones, but after a time the chess-players ate one each, and put one in Wang Chih's mouth, and he found it was not a date stone at all. It was a delicious kind of sweetmeat, the like of which he had never tasted before, and the strangest thing about it was that it took his hunger and thirst away.

He sat there some time longer, and noticed that as the old men frowned over the chessboard, their beards grew longer and longer, until they swept the floor of the cave, and even found their way out of the door.

"I hope my beard will never grow as quickly," said Wang Chih, as he rose, took up his axe again, and went down the mountain.

To his great shock, he found the fields where he had worked covered with houses, and a busy

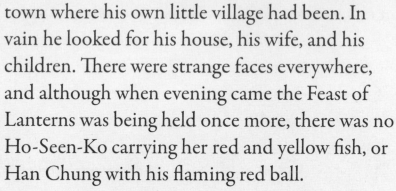

town where his own little village had been. In vain he looked for his house, his wife, and his children. There were strange faces everywhere, and although when evening came the Feast of Lanterns was being held once more, there was no Ho-Seen-Ko carrying her red and yellow fish, or Han Chung with his flaming red ball.

At last he found a woman, a very old woman, who told him that when she was a tiny girl she remembered her grandmother saying how, when she was a tiny girl, a poor young man had been spirited away by the genii of the mountains, on the day of the Feast of Lanterns, leaving his wife and little children with only a few handfuls of rice in the house. "Moreover, it has become a tradition in the procession for two children to be dressed to represent Han Chung and Ho-Seen-Ko, and a woman as their mother carrying the empty rice bowl between them, to remind people to take care of the widow and fatherless," she said.

Wang Chih's heart was heavy and he walked

out of the town. He slept on the mountain, and
early in the morning found his way back to the
cave where the two old men were playing chess.

"You must go to the White Hare of the Moon,
and ask him for a bottle of the elixir of life. If you
drink that you will live forever," said one of them.

"But I don't want to live forever," objected
Wang Chih. "I wish to go back and live in the
days when my wife and children were here."

"Ah! For that you must mix the elixir of life
with some water out of the sky-dragon's mouth."

"And where is the sky-dragon to be found?"
enquired Wang Chih.

"In the sky, of course. He lives in a cloud-cave.
And when he comes out of it he breathes fire, and
sometimes water. If he is breathing fire you will be
burned up, but if it is water, you will be able to
catch some in a bottle. What else do you want?"

"I want a pair of wings to fly with, and a bottle
to catch the water in," Wang Chih replied boldly.
So they gave him a bottle, and before he had

293

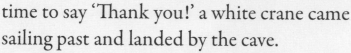

time to say 'Thank you!' a white crane came sailing past and landed by the cave.

"The crane will take you wherever you like," said the old men. "Go now, and leave us in peace."

So Wang Chih sat on the white crane's back, and was taken to the cloud-cave where the sky-dragon lived. When he got there, he sat near the cave, and thought how to bring the dragon out, and make him breathe water instead of fire.

"I have it!" cried Wang Chih. He struck a light and set the grass on fire, and the flames spread all around the entrance to the cave, and made such a smoke and crackling that the sky-dragon put his head out to see what was the matter. The dragon had the head of a camel, the horns of a deer, the eyes of a rabbit, the ears of a cow and the claws of a hawk. Besides this, he had whiskers and a beard, and in his beard were pearls.

"Ho ho!" cried the dragon, when he saw what Wang Chih had done, "I can soon put this to rights." And he breathed once, and the water

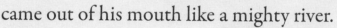

came out of his mouth like a mighty river.

Wang Chih, who had taken care to fill his bottle when the first stream began to flow, sailed away on the white crane's back as fast as he could, to escape being drowned.

The rivers poured over the cloud rock, until there was not a spark of fire left alight, and rushed down through the sky into the sea below.

Meanwhile, Wang Chih was on his way to the moon, and when he got there he went straight to the hut where the hare of the moon lived, and knocked at the door.

The hare was busy pounding the drugs that make up the elixir of life, but he left his work, and opened the door, and invited Wang Chih to come in. He was not ugly, like the dragon. His fur was quite white and soft and glossy, and he had lovely, gentle brown eyes. As soon as he heard what Wang Chih wanted, he opened two windows at the back of the hut, and told him to look through each of them in turn. "Tell me what

you see," said the hare, going back to the table where he was pounding the drugs.

"I can see a great many houses and people," said Wang Chih, "and streets – why, this is the town I was in yesterday, the one which has taken the place of my old village."

"Do you want to go back there?" asked the wise old hare.

Wang Chih shook his head.

"Then close the window. It is the window of the Present. And look through the other, which is the window of the Past."

Wang Chih obeyed, and through this window he saw his own dear little village, and his wife, and Han Chung and Ho-Seen-Ko jumping about her as she hung up the coloured lanterns outside the door.

Wang Chih turned, and looked eagerly at the White Hare. "Please let me go to them," he said desperately. "I have water from the sky-dragon's mouth, and—"

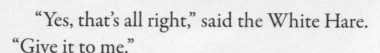

"Yes, that's all right," said the White Hare. "Give it to me."

He opened the bottle and mixed the contents carefully with a few drops of the elixir of life, which was clear as crystal, and of which each drop shone like a diamond as he poured it in.

"Now, drink this," he said to Wang Chih, "and it will give you the power of living once more in the past, as you desire."

Wang Chih held out his hand and drank every drop of the mixture.

The moment he had done so, the window grew larger, and he saw some steps leading from it down into the village street. Thanking the hare, he rushed through it and ran toward his own house, arriving in time to take the taper from his wife's hand with which she was about to light the red and yellow lanterns that swung over the door.

"What has kept you so long, Father? Where have you been?" asked Han Chung, while little Ho-Seen-Ko wondered why he kissed and

embraced them all so eagerly.

But Wang Chih did not tell them his
adventures just then, and only when darkness fell,
and the Feast of Lanterns began, he took his part
in it with a merry heart.

The Old Man and the Gift

From *Japanese Fairy Tales* by Yei Theodora Ozaki

Long ago there lived an old man and his wife who supported themselves by farming a small plot of land. Their life had been happy and peaceful save for one great sorrow – they had no child. They lavished all their affection on their pet dog, Shiro – even giving him more to eat than they had themselves.

One day the old man heard Shiro barking in the field at the back of the house. He hurried out to see what was the matter with him. Shiro ran to meet him, and, seizing the end of his kimono, dragged him under a large yenoki tree. Here he began to dig as fast as he could, yelping with joy. The old man ran back to the house,

fetched his spade and joined Shiro in digging. Imagine his astonishment when he came upon a heap of old and valuable coins. He and his wife were rich!

Now, the old man had a horrible neighbour, and he did not notice that this nasty man was peering in through the bamboo hedge and had seen everything. This neighbour began to think that he, too, would like to find a fortune. So a few

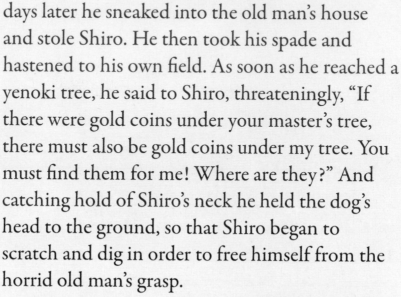

days later he sneaked into the old man's house and stole Shiro. He then took his spade and hastened to his own field. As soon as he reached a yenoki tree, he said to Shiro, threateningly, "If there were gold coins under your master's tree, there must also be gold coins under my tree. You must find them for me! Where are they?" And catching hold of Shiro's neck he held the dog's head to the ground, so that Shiro began to scratch and dig in order to free himself from the horrid old man's grasp.

The old man was very pleased, for he at once supposed that some gold coins also lay buried under his tree. He pushed Shiro away and began to dig. Soon there was a foul smell and he came upon a stinking, rotting, rubbish heap. The old man was utterly disgusted! But this soon gave way to anger. He stormed back on to his neighbour's land and set fire to the yenoki tree under which Shiro had found the coins.

Imagine Shiro's master's horror when he saw

that his tree was ablaze! In a panic, he and his wife ran to fetch water to put out the flames. But by the time they quenched the fire, the tree was charred and dead. The old man cut it down and saved an unburned, thick, sturdy branch. He hollowed it out and made a bowl. He thought that his wife could use it for making rice cakes in, to offer to the gods in thanks for their blessings.

But no sooner had his wife begun to pound the rice, than it began to grow and grow till it was about five times the original amount, and the cakes were turned out of the bowl as if an invisible hand were at work. The old man and his wife tasted the cakes and found them nicer than any other food. So from this time they never troubled about food, they lived upon the cakes with which the bowl never ceased to supply.

The greedy neighbour, hearing this new piece of good luck, was filled with envy as before, and called on the old man to borrow the wonderful bowl. The old man was too kind to refuse.

Several days passed and the neighbour did not bring the bowl back, so Shiro's master went to ask for it. He found his neighbour sitting by a wood fire. The wicked neighbour said haughtily, "Have you come to ask me for your bowl? When I tried to pound cakes in it only some horrid smelling stuff came out. So I broke it into pieces and now I am burning it."

The good old man calmly said, "If you had asked me for the cakes, I would have given you as many as ever you wanted. Now please give me my bowl – even though it is but ashes."

The neighbour grudgingly agreed, and the old man carried home a basket full of ashes. Just as he reached his garden, a gust of wind blew some onto his trees. It was late autumn and all the trees had shed their leaves, but no sooner did the ashes

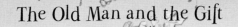

touch their branches than
the cherry trees, the plum trees,
and all the blossoming shrubs
burst into bloom, so that the old
man's garden was suddenly
transformed into a picture of spring.
The story of the old man's beautiful garden
spread far and wide. It even reached the ears
of a great earl, who had a prized cherry tree
that was mysteriously withering and dying.
The earl summoned the old man to his
palace to see if he could cure the tree. Of
course, as soon as the old man scattered some
ashes over it, it at once burst into full bloom!
The earl was so overjoyed that he
rewarded Shiro's master
with many riches. He also
gave him the title of Hana-Saka-Jijii, or 'The Old
Man who makes the Trees to Blossom', and sent
him home with great honour.
The wicked neighbour heard of the good old

man's fortune and was filled with jealousy. He gathered together all the ashes that remained in the fireplace from the burning of the wonderful bowl and went to the palace to tell the earl that he could revive dying plants too. The curious earl put him to the test – but the nasty neighbour's ashes did nothing to cure dying plants. In fact, they caused blossoming plants to die! The furious earl ordered the liar to be thrown into prison – and thus the nasty neighbour met with punishment at last for all his evil doings.

The good old man, however, with the treasure of coins and with all the gold and the silver which the earl had showered on him, became a rich and prosperous man in his old age, and lived a long and very happy life, with his good wife and his faithful dog, Shiro.

The Well of the World's End

From *English Fairy Tales*
by Joseph Jacobs

Once upon a time, there was a girl whose mother had died, and her father married again. And her stepmother hated her because she was more beautiful than herself. She used to make her do all the work, and never let her have any peace.

One day, the stepmother decided to get rid of her for good. She handed her a sieve and said, "Fill this at the Well of the World's End and bring it to me full, or woe betide you." The stepmother thought the girl would never be able to find the

307

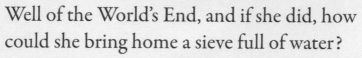

Well of the World's End, and if she did, how could she bring home a sieve full of water?

Well, the girl started off, and asked everyone she met where the Well of the World's End was. But nobody knew, and she didn't know what to do, when a little old woman, all bent double, told her how to get to it. So at last she arrived there, but when she dipped the sieve in the cold, cold water, it all ran out again. She tried and tried, but every time it was the same, and at last she sat down and cried as if her heart would break.

Suddenly she heard a croak, and she looked up and saw a frog with big eyes looking at her.

"What's the matter, dearie?" it said.

The girl explained, and the frog replied, "If you promise to do whatever I bid you for a whole night long, I'll tell you how to fill the sieve."

The girl didn't like the idea, but she had no choice, so she agreed. And the frog said,

"Stop it with moss and daub it with clay,
And then it will carry the water away."

Then it gave a hop, skip and jump – back into the Well of the World's End.

So the girl lined the sieve with moss, and over that she put some clay, and then she dipped it once again into the Well of the World's End, and this time, the water didn't run out.

Quite forgetting her promise to the frog, she went back to her stepmother, who was angry as angry, but said nothing at all.

That very evening they heard something tap-tapping at the door low down, and a voice cried out, "Open the door, my darling!"

The girl went and opened the door and, to her dismay, there was the frog from the Well of the World's End. She explained about the agreement, and her stepmother said, "Girls must keep their promises!" For she was quite gleeful that the girl would have to obey a nasty frog.

And it hopped, and it hopped, and it jumped, till it was right inside and then it said, "Let me sit on your knee, my dear!"

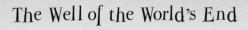

But the girl didn't like to, till her stepmother said, "Lift it up this instant! Girls must keep their promises!"

So at last she lifted the frog up on to her lap, and it lay there for a time, till at last it said, "Give me some supper, my sweetheart!"

Well, she didn't mind doing that, so she got it a bowl of milk and bread, and fed it well. And when the frog had finished, it said, "Now, go with me to bed, my own one!"

But that the girl wouldn't do, till her stepmother said, "Do what you promised, or out you go, you and your froggie."

So the girl took the frog with her to bed, and kept it as far away from her as she could. Well, just as the day was beginning to break what should the frog say but, "Chop off my head, my true love. Remember the promise you made to me!"

At first the girl wouldn't, for she thought of what the frog had done for her at the Well of the World's End. But when the frog said the words again, she took an axe and chopped off its head.

Lo and behold! There stood before her a handsome young prince, who told her that he had been enchanted by a wicked magician, and he could never be unspelled till some girl would do his bidding for a whole night, and chop off his head at the end of it.

So the prince and the girl were married and went away to live in the castle of the king, his father, and the stepmother hated every bit of it!

The Crystal Coffin

From Andrew Lang's *Green Fairy Book*

Ayoung tailor once found himself lost in a wood. Evening came on and, for fear of wild beasts, he climbed a tall oak tree. After passing several hours in fear, he noticed a light shining in the distance. Cautiously, he climbed down and went towards it.

The tailor found it came from a house, and he knocked bravely at the door. It was opened by an old man who said roughly, "Who are you, and what do you want?"

"I beg you to let me shelter in your hut till

morning," replied the youth.

Very grudgingly, the old man let him come in, and after giving him some bread and water, showed him to a bed in one corner of the room.

The weary tailor slept sound till early morning, when he was roused by a thunderous, bellowing noise. The tailor hurried out to find a huge black bull fighting with a fine large stag. At length, the stag drove his antlers with such force into his opponent's body that the bull fell to the ground, finished. Then, to the tailor's great amazement, the stag bounded up to him, forked him up with its great antlers, and set off at full gallop over hill and dale. The tailor could do

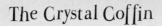

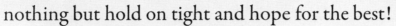

nothing but hold on tight and hope for the best!

At length the stag paused before a steep rock and let the tailor down to the ground. With his antlers, he struck such a blow on a door in the rock that it flew open. Flames of fire rushed forth and clouds of steam. The tailor was quite frozen with fear, but a voice from the rock cried, "Step in, no harm shall befall you."

Passing through the door, the tailor was amazed to find himself in a hall, whose ceiling, walls, and floor were covered with carved tiles.

Full of wonder, he heard the same voice saying, "Tread on the stone in the middle of the hall, and good luck will attend you."

Hardly had he stepped on the stone than it began to sink with him into the depths below. He found himself in an even more splendid hall,

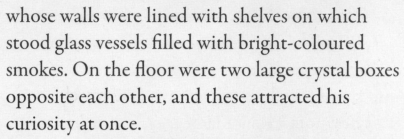

whose walls were lined with shelves on which
stood glass vessels filled with bright-coloured
smokes. On the floor were two large crystal boxes
opposite each other, and these attracted his
curiosity at once.

Stepping up to one, he saw within it a model
castle surrounded by farms, barns, stables, and a
number of other buildings. Everything was quite
tiny, but perfect.

He was even more amazed at what was in the
other crystal box. Lying there was a beautiful girl.
She looked asleep, but though her eyes were
closed, the bright colour in her face, and the
movement of a ribbon, which rose and fell with
her breath, left no doubt as to her being alive.

Suddenly the maiden opened her eyes and
started with delight. "Help me!" she cried. "Only
push back the bolt of this coffin and I am free
from my prison."

The tailor promptly obeyed, and the girl
quickly pushed back the crystal lid and stepped

out. After giving her rescuer a kiss to thank him, she explained, "I am the daughter of a wealthy nobleman. My parents died when I was very young, and they left me to the care of my eldest brother, whom I love very much.

"One evening, a stranger rode up to the castle and asked for shelter. Of course, we took him in. But that night, I woke to find the stranger entering my room, even though the door had been securely locked. He was softly singing a strange song, and I found I could neither move nor cry out! Then I must have fainted, for I remember nothing more until I opened my eyes to find myself lying here, in this crystal coffin.

"The magician – for that is indeed what the stranger was – appeared again and told me that he had transformed my brother into a wild stag. He had shrunk our castle and the surrounding village to miniature and locked them up in another glass box. And after turning everyone in our household into smoke, had banished them

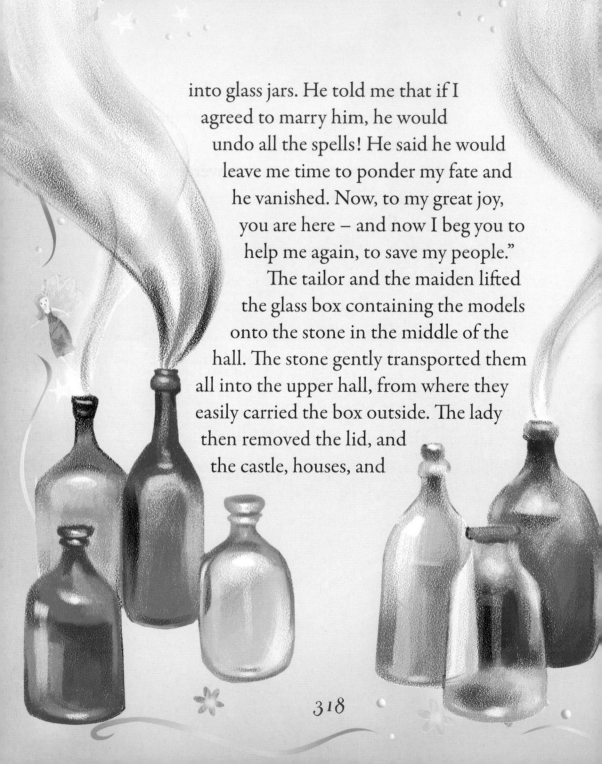

into glass jars. He told me that if I
agreed to marry him, he would
undo all the spells! He said he would
leave me time to ponder my fate and
he vanished. Now, to my great joy,
you are here – and now I beg you to
help me again, to save my people."

The tailor and the maiden lifted
the glass box containing the models
onto the stone in the middle of the
hall. The stone gently transported them
all into the upper hall, from where they
easily carried the box outside. The lady
then removed the lid, and
the castle, houses, and

farmyards grew and spread themselves till they had regained their proper size. Then the young couple brought up all the glass vessels filled with smoke. No sooner were they uncorked than brightly-coloured clouds billowed out of them and became all the lady's servants and attendants.

The maiden's joy was complete when her brother came from the forest in his proper shape. Of course, he had been the stag, and he had killed the magician – who had been in the form of the bull. That very day, the lady gave her hand in marriage to the young tailor, and they lived happily ever after.

The Baker's Daughter 322

Grasp All, Lose All 327

The Three Dwarves 337

MYSTERIOUS MORALS

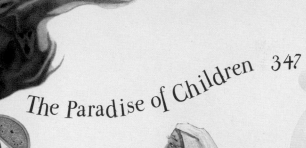

The Paradise of Children   347

The Hermit   358

Peter and the Magic Goose   370

The Baker's Daughter

From *Folk-lore and Legends*
by Charles John Tibbits

A long time ago, there lived a baker who was a mean, greedy man. He sought in every way to put money by, and cheated people whenever he was able when they came to his shop. He had a daughter who helped him in his business, and seeing how her father treated the people, and how he succeeded in getting money by his bad practices, she, too, in time came to do the like.

One day when her father was away, and the girl remained alone in the shop, an old woman came in. "My pretty girl," said she, "give me a bit of dough I beg of you, for I am old and very hungry."

The girl at first told her to be off, but as the old woman would not go, and begged harder than before for a piece of bread, at last the baker's daughter took up a piece of dough, and giving it to her, said, "There now, be off, and do not trouble me any more."

"My dear," said the woman, "you have given me a piece of dough, let me bake it in your oven, for I have no place of my own to bake it in."

"Very well," replied the girl, and, taking the dough, she placed it in the oven, while the old woman sat down to wait till it was baked.

When the girl thought the bread should be ready she looked in the oven expecting to find a small cake, and was much amazed to find instead a very large loaf of bread. She pretended to look about the oven as if in search of something.

"I cannot find the cake," said she. "It must have

tumbled into the fire and got burned."

"Very well," said the old woman, "give me another piece of dough instead and I will wait while it bakes."

So the girl took another piece of dough, smaller than the first piece, and having put it in the oven, shut the door. At the end of a few minutes or so she looked in again, and found there another loaf, larger than the last. "Dear me," said she, pretending to look about her, "I have surely lost the dough again. There's no cake here."

"Tis a pity," said the old woman, "but never mind. I will wait while you bake another piece."

So the baker's daughter took some dough as small as one of her fingers and put it in the oven, while the old woman sat near. When she thought it ought to be baked, she looked in the oven and saw a loaf, larger than either of the others.

"That is mine," said the old woman.

"No," replied the girl. "How could such a large loaf have grown out of a little piece of dough?"

"It is mine, I am sure," said the woman.

"It is not," said the girl. "You shall not have it."

Well, when the old woman saw that the girl would not give her the loaf, and saw how she had tried to cheat her – for she was a fairy, and knew all the tricks that the baker's daughter had put upon her – she drew out from under her cloak a stick, and just touched the girl with it. Then a wonderful thing occurred, for the girl suddenly changed into an owl, and flying about the room, at last, made for the door, and, finding it open, she flew out and was never seen again.

Grasp All, Lose All

From Andrew Lang's *Olive Fairy Book*

Once, in former times, there lived in a city in India a poor oil-seller, called Déna. He had borrowed from a banker, of the name of Léna, the sum of one hundred rupees, which, with the interest Léna charged, amounted to a debt of three hundred rupees. Now Déna had no money to pay his debt, so Léna was angry and threatened to punish him. One day, Déna decided that he had no choice but to run away. So that evening, he told his wife, and slipped out of the city without knowing where he was going.

At about ten o'clock that night Déna came to a well by the wayside, near which grew a giant peepul tree. As he was very tired, he climbed up into it and settled down to rest there for the night. Whilst he slept, some spirits, which roam about such places on certain nights, picked up the tree and flew away with it to a faraway shore where no creature lived, and there, long before the sun rose, they set it down.

Just then the oil-seller awoke, and was amazed to behold nothing but waste shore and wide sea, and was dumb with horror and astonishment. Whilst he sat up, trying to collect his senses, he began to catch sight

328

here and there of
twinkling, flashing lights, like
little fires, that moved and
sparkled all about, and wondered
what they were. Presently he saw
one so close to him that he
reached out his hand and
grasped it, and found that it was
a sparkling red stone, scarcely
smaller than a walnut. He opened a
corner of his loin-cloth and tied the
stone in it. By-and-by he got another, and
then a third, and a fourth, all of which he tied
up carefully in his cloth. At last, just as the day
was breaking, the tree rose, and, flying
rapidly through the air, was deposited once
more by the well where it had stood the
previous evening.

When Déna had recovered a little from
the fright, he made his way back to the city and
to his own house. After carefully shutting all the

doors, he opened the corner of his loin-cloth and showed the four stones, which glittered and flashed as he turned them over and over.

"Pooh!" said his wife. "What use are such silly, small pebbles! Now if you had found food or money, there'd be some sense in it!" And she turned away with a sniff.

Just then, Léna threw open the door and demanded his money.

Déna politely invited the moneylender in, carefully shut the door as before, and then showed him the four great flashing stones. "This is all," said he, "that I have in the world to set against my debt, for, as your honour knows, I haven't a penny, but the stones are pretty!"

Now Léna saw at once that the stones were in fact magnificent rubies, and his mouth watered for want of them, but as it would never do to show what was in his mind, he went on, "What do I care about your stupid stones? It is my money I want, my lawful debt that you owe me, and I shall get it out of you yet somehow or another, or it will be so much the worse for you."

And so Léna went on and on, while Déna begged for mercy – until, at length, Léna very grudgingly announced that he would take the stones instead of the money. Whilst Déna nearly wept with gratitude, he wrote out a receipt for the three hundred rupees, and, wrapping the four stones in a cloth, he put them into his jacket. He hurried off to the house of the chief wazir to do a deal to exchange them for money. Before long, he had given the rubies to the chief wazir and was striding home with ten thousand rupees in his pocket, quite overjoyed.

The chief wazir was quite stunned by the beauty of the rubies and went straight away to the palace, to show them to his royal master, the rajah.

"Oh, ho!" said the rajah. "These are truly priceless gems, and you have done well to give them to me. In return I will make you the master of ten villages."

Whilst the rajah put the rubies into his turban, the chief wazir hurried away beaming with happiness at the thought that for ten thousand rupees he had become lord of ten villages.

The rajah was also equally pleased, and strolled off with his new purchases to the women's quarters and showed them to the queen, who was nearly out of her mind with delight. Then, as she turned them over and over in her hands, she said, "Ah! If I had eight more such gems, what a necklace they would make! Get me eight more of them or I shall die!" And then she fell to weeping and wailing until the rajah promised that in the morning he would make arrangements to get some more such rubies.

In the morning the rajah sent for the wazir, and said that he must manage to get eight more rubies like those he had brought him the day before, "And if you don't I shall hang you," cried the rajah, for he was very cross.

The wazir left the palace, much troubled in mind, and bade his slaves bring Léna before him. "Get me eight more such rubies as those you brought yesterday," commanded the wazir. "Eight more, and be quick, or I am a dead man."

"But how?" wailed Léna. "I got them from Déna, the oil-seller, and they were all he had."

"Well, send for him and ask him where he got them," answered the wazir. And more slaves were sent to summon Déna.

When Déna arrived he was closely questioned, and then all three went to see the rajah, and to him Déna told the whole story.

"What night was it that you slept in the peepul tree?" demanded the rajah.

"I can't remember," said Déna, "but my wife will be able to tell you."

Then Déna's wife was sent for, and she explained that it was on the last Sunday of the new moon. Now everyone knows that it is on the Sunday of the new moon that spirits have special

333

power to play pranks upon mortals. So the rajah forbade them all, on pain of death, to say a word to anyone, and declared that, on the next Sunday of the new moon, they four – the rajah, the wazir, Léna and Déna – would go and sit in the peepul tree and see what happened.

The days dragged on to the appointed Sunday, and that evening the four met secretly, and entered the forest. They had not far to go before they reached the peepul tree, into which they climbed as the rajah had planned. At midnight the tree began to sway, and presently away it flew, with the four men clinging tightly to its branches, until at last it was set down by the waste seashore where a great wide sea came tumbling in on a desert beach. Presently, as before, they began to see little points of light that glistened like fires all around them.

Then Déna thought to himself, 'Think! Last time I only took four that came close to me, and I got rid of all my debt in return. This time I will take all I can get and be rich!'

'If I got ten thousand rupees for four stones,' thought Léna, 'I will gather forty now for myself, and become so wealthy that they will probably make me a wazir at least!'

'For four stones I received ten villages,' the wazir was silently thinking to himself. 'Now I will get stones enough to purchase an entire kingdom, and I will become a rajah and employ wazirs of my very own!'

And the rajah thought to himself, 'What is the good of only getting eight stones to make one necklace? Why, here there are enough stones to make at least twenty necklaces, and that much wealth means power!'

Full of greed, each man scrambled down from the tree, spread his cloth, and darted hither and thither picking up the precious jewels, looking all the while over his shoulder to see whether his neighbour fared better than he. So engrossed were they in the business of gathering wealth that

the dawn arrived, and before they knew it the tree rose up again and flew away, leaving them on the seashore staring after it, each with his cloth heavy with priceless jewels.

In palace, the chamberlains declared that the rajah had gone out the evening before and not returned. They waited and searched – but none of the men returned, and the tale told by Déna's wife was the only clue to their fate.

To this day, in that country, people warn greedy folk: "If you reach for more, you may well lose everything!"

The Three Dwarves

From Andrew Lang's *Red Fairy Book*

There was once a man who lost his wife, and a woman who lost her husband. The man had a daughter and so had the woman. The two girls were friends and used often to play together. One day the woman turned to the man's daughter and said, "Go and tell your father that I will marry him, and then he will be better looked after."

The girl went home and told her father what the woman had said.

"What am I to do?" he answered. Not being

able to make up his mind, he took off his boot, and handing it to his daughter, said, "Take this boot which has a hole in the sole, hang it up on a nail in the hayloft, and pour water into it. If it holds water I will marry again, but if it doesn't I won't."

The girl did as she was bid, but the water drew the hole together and the boot filled up to the very top. She went and told her father the result, and he got up and went to see for himself. When he saw that it was true and that there was no mistake, he accepted his fate, proposed to the widow, and they were married at once.

On the morning after the wedding, when the two girls awoke, milk was standing for the man's daughter to wash in and wine for her to drink, but for the woman's daughter, only water to wash in and only water to drink. On the second morning, water to wash in and water to drink was standing for the man's daughter as well. And on the third morning, water to wash in and water to drink was standing for the man's daughter, and milk to wash in and wine to drink for the woman's daughter. And so it continued ever after. The woman hated her stepdaughter from the bottom of her heart, and did all she could to make her life miserable. She was as jealous as she could possibly be, because the girl was so beautiful and charming, while her own daughter was both ugly and repulsive.

One winter's day when there was a hard frost, and mountain and valley were covered with snow, the woman made a dress of paper, and calling the girl to her said, "Put on this dress and go into the wood and fetch me a basket of strawberries!"

"Now heaven help us," replied her stepdaughter, "strawberries don't grow in winter – the earth is all frozen and the snow has covered everything up. And why send me out in a paper dress? It is so cold outside that one's very breath freezes – the wind will whistle through my dress, and the brambles tear it from my body."

"How dare you contradict me!" said her stepmother. "Be off with you at once, and don't show your face again till you have filled the basket with strawberries." Then she gave her a hard crust of bread, saying, "That will be enough for you today." And she thought to herself, 'The girl will certainly perish of hunger and cold, and I shan't be bothered with her any more.'

The girl was so obedient that she put on the paper dress and set out with her little basket. There was nothing but snow far and near, and not a green blade of grass anywhere. When she came to the wood she saw a little house, and out of it peeped three dwarfs. She wished them good day, and knocked at the door. They called out to her to enter, so she stepped in and sat down on a seat by the fire, wishing to warm herself and eat her breakfast. The dwarfs said at once, "Give us some of your food!"

"Gladly," she said, and breaking her crust in two, she gave them the half.

Then they asked her what she was doing in the depths of winter in her thin dress.

"Oh," she answered, "I have been sent to get a basketful of strawberries, and I daren't show my face again at home till I bring them with me."

When she had finished her bread they gave her a broom and told her to sweep away the snow from the back door. As soon as she left the room to do so, the three little men consulted what they should give her as a reward for being so sweet and good, and for sharing her last crust with them.

The first said, "Every day she shall grow prettier."

The second, "Every time she opens her mouth a piece of gold shall fall out."

And the third, "A king shall marry her."

The girl in the meantime was doing as the dwarfs had bidden her, and was sweeping the snow away from the back door, and what do you think she found there? Heaps of fine ripe strawberries that showed out dark red against the

white snow. She joyfully picked enough to fill her basket, thanked the little men for their kindness, shook hands with them, and ran home to bring her stepmother what she had asked for.

As she walked in and said, "Good evening," a piece of gold fell out of her mouth. Then she told what had happened in the wood, and at every word pieces of gold dropped from her mouth, so the room was soon covered with them.

"She's surely more money than wit to throw gold about like that," said her stepsister, but in her secret heart she was very jealous, and determined that she too would go to the wood and look for strawberries.

But her mother refused to let her go, saying, "My dear child, it is far too cold, you might freeze to death."

The girl however left her no peace, so she was forced at last to give in, but she insisted on her putting on a beautiful fur cloak, and she gave her bread and butter and cakes to eat on the way.

The girl went straight to the little house in the wood, and as before the three little men were looking out of the window. She took no notice of them, and without as much as 'By your leave' or 'With your leave' she flounced into the room, sat herself down at the fire, and began to eat her bread and butter and cakes.

"Give us some!" cried the dwarfs.

But she answered, "No, I won't, it's hardly enough for myself!"

When she had finished eating they said, "There's a broom for you, go and clear up our back door."

"Do it yourselves, I'm not your servant," she answered rudely.

When she saw that they did not mean to give her anything, she left the house in no amiable frame of mind. Then the three little men consulted about what they should do to her, because she was

343

so rude and had such a greedy nature, that she grudged everybody their good fortune.

The first said, "She shall grow uglier every day."

The second, "Every time she speaks, a toad shall jump out of her mouth."

And the third, "She will be left lonely."

The girl searched for strawberries, but she found none, and returned home in a very bad temper. When she opened her mouth to tell her mother what had happened, a toad jumped out, so everyone was quite disgusted with her.

Then the stepmother was more furious than ever, and from then on she did nothing but plot mischief against the man's daughter, who was daily growing more and more beautiful. At last, one day the wicked woman took a large pot, put it on the fire and boiled some yarn in it. When it was well scalded she hung it round the poor girl's shoulder and, giving her an axe, she bade her break a hole in the frozen river, and rinse the yarn in it. Her stepdaughter obeyed as usual, and went and broke a hole in the ice. While she was busily engaged in wringing out the yarn a magnificent carriage passed, and the king sat inside. The carriage stood still, and the king asked her, "My child, who are you, and what in the wide world are you doing here?"

"I am only a poor girl," she answered, "and am rinsing out my yarn in the river."

Then the king was sorry for her, and when he saw how beautiful she was he said, "Will you come away with me?"

"Gladly," she said, for she knew how willingly she would leave her stepmother and sister, and how glad they would be to be rid of her.

So she stepped into the carriage and drove away with the king, and when they reached his palace the wedding was celebrated with much splendour. So all turned out just as the three little dwarfs had said.

The Paradise of Children

From *A Wonder-Book for Girls and Boys*
by Nathaniel Hawthorne

Long, long ago, there was a boy named Epimetheus who didn't have a best friend – until he met a girl called Pandora. The first time Pandora went to Epimetheus's house, she noticed a curious, great box. And almost the first question she put to him, after crossing the threshold, was, "Epimetheus, what have you in that box?"

"That is a secret," answered Epimetheus, "and you must not ask any questions about it. The box was left here to be kept safely, and I do not myself know what it contains."

347

"But who gave it to you?" asked Pandora. "And where did it come from?"

"That is a secret, too," replied Epimetheus.

"How vexing!" exclaimed Pandora, pouting.

"Oh, come, don't think of it any more," cried Epimetheus. "Let's go and play with the other children."

It is thousands of years since Epimetheus and Pandora were alive, and the world, nowadays, is very different from in their time. Then, everybody was a child. They needed no fathers and mothers because there was no danger, nor trouble of any kind, and no clothes to be mended, and there was always plenty to eat and drink. It was a very pleasant life indeed. No jobs to be done, no schoolwork to be studied – there was nothing but games and dancing and singing and laughter. For what was most wonderful of all, the children never quarrelled or cried or sulked. The truth is, those ugly little winged monsters, called Troubles, which are now almost as numerous as mosquitoes, had never yet been seen on the earth. It is probable that the very greatest annoyance that a child had ever experienced was Pandora's vexation at not being able to discover the secret of the mysterious box. This was at first only the faint shadow of a Trouble, but every day it grew more and more.

"Where can the box have come from?" Pandora continually kept saying to herself. "And what in the world can be inside it?" One day she begged Epimetheus to tell her more about how the box came to be in his house.

"It was just left at the door," replied Epimetheus, "by a person dressed in an odd kind of a cloak, and a cap that seemed to be made partly of feathers, so that it looked almost as if it had wings. He had a curious walking staff – it was like two serpents twisting around a stick, and was carved so naturally that I, at first, thought the serpents were alive. He told me very sternly that until he comes back and gives permission, no one has any right to lift the lid of the box."

Then, quite fed up of thinking about the box, Epimetheus went out to play.

Pandora, who had refused to go with him, was left gazing at the box. It was made of a beautiful kind of wood, so highly polished that she could see her face in it. The edges and corners were carved with most wonderful skill. There were figures of graceful men and women, and the prettiest children ever seen, surrounded by a tangle of flowers and leaves. Once or twice as Pandora examined it, she fancied that she saw a face not so lovely, or something or other that was disagreeable. Nevertheless, on looking more closely, and touching the spot with her finger, she could discover nothing of the kind.

The most beautiful face of all was in the centre of the lid. Pandora thought that, had it been able to speak, it looked just as if it would have said,

"Do not be afraid, Pandora! What harm can there be in opening the box? Never mind that poor, simple Epimetheus! You are wiser than he, and have ten times as much spirit. Open the box, and see if you do not find something very pretty!"

The box was fastened by a very intricate knot of gold cord. There appeared to be no end to this knot, and no beginning. But Pandora was not one to give up easily. She stood for a while, turning it this way and that, and then murmured to herself, "I really believe that I begin to see how it was done. I am sure that if I undid it, I could do it up again afterwards."

She took the golden knot in her fingers, and was soon busily engaged in attempting to undo it. Meanwhile, the bright sunshine came through the open window, as did likewise the merry voices of the children, playing at a distance, and perhaps the voice of Epimetheus among them. Pandora stopped to listen. What a beautiful day it was! Would it not be wiser if she were to let the troublesome knot alone, and think no more about the box, but run and join her playfellows and be happy?

All this time, however, her fingers were half unconsciously busy with the knot, and just then, by the merest accident, she gave the knot a kind of twist. The gold cord untwined itself, as if by magic, and left the box without a fastening.

Suddenly Pandora seemed to hear the murmur of small voices within. "Let us out, dear Pandora – pray, let us out!"

'What can it be?' thought Pandora. 'Is there something alive in the box? Maybe I should take a peep – just one peep – and then the lid shall be shut down as safely as ever! There cannot possibly be any harm in having just one little peep!'

As Pandora raised the lid, the cottage grew very dark and dismal, for a black cloud had swept quite over the sun, and seemed to have buried it alive. There had for a little while past been a low growling and muttering, which all at once broke

into a heavy peal of thunder. But Pandora, heeding nothing of all this, lifted the lid nearly upright, and looked inside. It seemed as if a sudden swarm of winged creatures brushed past her, taking flight out of the box. At the same instant, she heard Epimetheus's footsteps returning and he cried out as if he were in pain.

"Oh, I am stung! I am stung! Pandora, why have you opened this wicked box?"

Pandora let fall the lid, and, starting up, looked about her, to see what had befallen Epimetheus. The thunder cloud had so darkened the room that she could not very clearly discern what was in it. But as her eyes grew more accustomed to the imperfect light, she saw a crowd of ugly little shapes, with bats' wings, looking horribly spiteful, and armed with terribly long stings in their tails. It was one of these that had stung Epimetheus. Nor was it a great while before Pandora herself was stung and she too began to scream in pain.

The ugly things that had made their escape out of the box were the whole family of earthly Troubles. There were evil Passions, there were a great many species of Cares, there were more than a hundred and fifty Sorrows, there were Diseases (in a vast number of miserable and painful shapes), there were more kinds of Naughtiness than it would be of any use to talk about. And now the evil Troubles flew out of the windows and doors, to pester and torment the children all over the world – who from that moment on began to grow old and die.

Meanwhile, Epimetheus sat down sullenly in a corner while Pandora flung herself upon the floor, sobbing as if her heart would break.

Suddenly there was a gentle little tap on the inside of the lid.

"What can that noise be?" cried Pandora, lifting her head.

Epimetheus made no answer.

Again the tap! It sounded like the tiny

knuckles of a fairy's hand, knocking lightly and playfully on the inside of the box. "Let me out!" came a sweet voice. "I am not like those wicked creatures that have stings in their tails. They are no brothers and sisters of mine, as you would see at once, if you were only to get a glimpse of me. Come, come, my pretty Pandora! I am sure you will let me out!"

"Shall I lift the lid again?" whispered Pandora to Epimetheus.

"Just as you please," replied the boy. "You have done so much mischief already, that perhaps you may as well do a little more. One other Trouble, in such a swarm as you have set adrift about the world, can make no very great difference."

So the two children again lifted the lid. Out flew a sunny and smiling little personage, and hovered about the room, throwing a light wherever she went. She flew to Epimetheus, and laid the least touch of her finger on the inflamed spot where the Trouble had stung him, and immediately the anguish of it was gone. Then she kissed Pandora on the forehead, and her hurt was cured likewise.

"Who are you, beautiful creature?" enquired Pandora, shyly.

"I am called Hope!" answered the sunshiny figure. " I was packed into the box, to make amends to the human race for that swarm of ugly Troubles, which was destined to be let loose among them. Never fear – we shall do pretty well in spite of them all."

"And will you stay with us," asked Epimetheus, "forever and ever?"

"As long as you need me," said Hope, "and that will be as long as you live in the world – I promise never to desert you."

And she never has.

The Hermit

From *Tales of Wonder Every Child Should Know*
by Kate Douglas Wiggin and
Nora Archibald Smith

*I*n the reign of King Moabdar there lived at Babylon a young man named Zadig. He was handsome, rich, and good-hearted. At the moment when this story opens, he was travelling to see the world and learn wisdom. However, he had seen so many terrible disasters and encountered so much misery among people that he had begun to think that the world was very unfair and to doubt that God existed. In this very unhappy state of mind he was walking on the banks of the River Euphrates, when he chanced to meet a holy hermit, whose snowy beard fell to his belt. He carried a scroll that he was reading very intently. Zadig stopped, bowed, and inquired what the scroll was.

"It is the Book of Destiny," replied the hermit. "Would you like to read it?"

He handed it to Zadig, but though Zadig knew a dozen languages, he could not understand a word of it. His curiosity increased.

"I can tell from your face that you are a troubled man," said the kindly hermit.

"Alas!" said Zadig. "I do feel very gloomy."

"Allow me to accompany you," said the hermit, "I may be useful to you. I am sometimes able to comfort the sorrowful."

Zadig was impressed by the holy appearance and the mysterious scroll of the old hermit, and thought that he must be very learned and wise. He was delighted that the old man wanted to accompany him. As they walked, the hermit spoke of fairness, of fate, of temptations and

human weaknesses, and of all the goodness in life, with so much power that Zadig was quite captivated and wanted to listen to him for as long as possible. He begged the hermit not to leave him until they returned to Babylon.

"I ask you the same favour," said the hermit. "Promise me that, whatever I may do, you will keep me company for several days."

Zadig gave the promise, and they journeyed onwards together.

That night the travellers arrived at a grand mansion. The hermit begged for food and

lodging for himself and his companion. The porter, who was so richly dressed that he might have been mistaken for a prince, ushered them in with a very snooty air. The chief servant showed them the magnificent apartments where they were to spend the night, and they were then admitted to the great hall to dine at the long, long dinner table – albeit they were sat at the very bottom, where the master of the mansion did not even cast a glance at them. They were, however, served with all sorts of delicious morsels, and, after dinner, washed their hands in a golden basin

set with emeralds and rubies. After an extremely comfortable night's sleep, the next morning, before they left the castle, a servant brought them each a piece of gold.

"The master of the house," said Zadig, as they went their way, "appears to be a generous man, although he obviously thinks too highly of himself." As he spoke he noticed that a kind of large pouch which the hermit carried appeared much bigger than usual. He asked what was in it and the hermit explained that it was the golden basin, set with precious stones, which he had stolen! Zadig was highly astonished – but he didn't say anything.

At noon the hermit stopped before a little house, in which lived a man who was very wealthy but very mean. An old valet in a shabby coat received them very rudely, showed them into the stable, and set before them a few rotten olives, some mouldy bread, and beer that had turned sour. However, the hermit didn't seem upset at all. In fact, he ate and drank with as much content as he had shown the night before. Then, addressing the old valet, who had kept his eye upon them to make sure that they stole nothing, he gave him the two gold pieces that they had received that morning, and thanked him for his kind attention. "Be so good," he added, "as to let me see your master."

The astonished valet showed them in.

"Most mighty sir," said the hermit, "I can only give you my humble thanks for the noble manner in which you have received us. I beseech you to accept this golden basin as a token of my gratitude."

The mean man almost fell backwards with amazement. The hermit, without waiting for him to recover, set off with speed with his companion.

"What does all this mean?" asked Zadig. "You steal a golden basin set with jewels from a man who receives you generously, and you give it to a curmudgeon who treats you badly."

"My son," replied the hermit, "I can assure you that from now on, the mighty lord who only welcomes travellers in order to display his riches, will grow wiser. However, the mean man will gradually be taught generosity. Be amazed at nothing, and follow me."

Zadig knew not whether he was dealing with the most foolish or the wisest of all men. But the hermit spoke with such faith that Zadig had no choice except to follow him.

That night they came to a simple but comfortable-looking house, with no signs of either showiness nor meanness. The owner was a wise man who had taken himself off to live by himself and study peacefully the rules of goodness and common sense, and who yet was happy and contented. He had built this calm house to suit himself, and he received the strangers in it with openness and straight-forwardness. He led them himself to a comfortable chamber, where he left the travellers to rest awhile. Then he returned to lead them to a dainty supper. They held an interesting conversation, during which they agreed that the wisest people are not always the ones in charge of the things that happen in the world. The hermit also made the point that the world is much bigger than we know and things often happen for reasons that we don't understand. Zadig wondered how it was that a person who committed such mad acts could seem to talk so sensibly!

At length, the host led the two travellers to their apartment, and thanked heaven for sending him two visitors who were so wise and good. He offered them some money, but the old man declined with thanks and bade their host goodnight.

At break of day the hermit woke his comrade. "We must be going," he remarked. "But while everyone is still asleep, I wish to leave this worthy man a gift." With these words he took a torch and

set the house on fire. Zadig burst forth into cries
of horror, and would have stopped the frightful
act, but the hermit was somehow stronger and
pushed him away. Beaten back by both the old
man and the heat, Zadig was forced to leave the
house in a blaze and retreat to a safe distance.

366

When the travellers were both a good way off, the hermit looked back calmly at the burning pile. "Heaven be praised!" he cried. "Our kind host's house is destroyed from top to bottom." At these words Zadig knew not whether he should burst out laughing, call the holy man an old rascal, knock him down, or run away. But he did none of these things. Still overwhelmed by the firm manner of the hermit, he followed him against his will to their next lodging.

This was the dwelling of a good and charitable widow, who had a nephew of fourteen, her only hope and joy. She did her best to treat the travellers well, and the next morning she bade her nephew guide them safely past a certain bridge, which, having recently been broken, had become dangerous to cross over. The youth, eager to oblige them, led the way.

"Come," said the hermit, when they were half across the bridge, "I must show my gratitude towards your aunt," and as he spoke he seized the

young man by the hair and threw him into the river. The youth fell, reappeared for an instant on the surface, and then was swallowed by the torrent.

"Oh, monster!" exclaimed Zadig. "Ah! Most evil of men—"

"You promised me more patience," interrupted the old man. "Listen! Beneath the ruins of that house that I set on fire, the owner will discover an enormous treasure, while this young man, whose existence I cut short, would have turned to wickedness and killed his aunt within a year, and you yourself in two."

"Who told you so?" cried Zadig. "Even if you read this in your Book of Destiny, who bestowed upon you the power to drown a youth who never harmed you?"

Once he had spoken, he saw that the old man had a beard no longer, and that his face had become young. His hermit's frock had disappeared, and four white wings covered his back and shone with dazzling light.

"You are an angel of heaven!" cried Zadig.

"People," replied the angel Jezrael, for that's who he was, "judge all things without true knowledge, and you, of all people, most deserved help to become wise. The world imagines that the youth who has just died fell by accident into the water, and that by similar accident the rich man's house was set on fire. But there is no such thing as chance – everything happens to test people or to punish people or because of things that must happen in the future."

As he spoke, the angel flew up to heaven, and Zadig fell upon his knees.

Peter and the Magic Goose

From *Fairy Stories and Fables*
by James Baldwin

There was once a man who had three sons. The eldest of these sons was called Jacob, the second John, and the youngest Peter. Now Peter was good-natured and not very wise, and so it was easy for his brothers to play tricks on him. When there was hard work to be done, it was Peter that had to do it, and when anything went wrong about the farm, it was Peter that had to bear the blame for it.

One day in summer, Jacob wanted to go into the woods to cut down a tree. So his mother gave

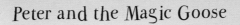

him a nice cake and a bottle of milk
for lunch, and told him that as soon
as he felt tired he must come home
and let Peter finish the job.

While he was looking at the
trees and wondering which
one to cut down, a
little red-faced man
came along. He
seemed to be very old
and feeble, and he
said to Jacob, "Kind
sir, will you not give
me a piece of
that nice
cake that is in your pocket?
I have not had anything to eat
since yesterday."

"Not a bit of it," said Jacob. "I have
nothing for beggars. If you want food,
you must work for it as I do."

371

The little man said not a word but hobbled away, and Jacob began to chop his tree. He had hardly made a dozen strokes when his foot slipped. He fell against his axe and cut his arm so badly that he had to go home to have it bound.

The next day John said that he would go out and finish cutting the tree. So his mother baked a nice cake for him, and gave him a bottle of milk for his lunch, and told him to take care and not hurt himself.

John had hardly reached the wood, when he met the little red-faced man, hobbling along among the trees. "Please give me a bite of the nice cake and let me have a taste of the milk in that bottle," said the man, "for I am almost dead with hunger and thirst."

"Why should I give you anything?" said John, "I have no more than I want for myself."

The little man made no answer, and John walked on through the woods, until he found the tree that his brother had begun to chop down. At the very first stroke, his axe glanced and struck his foot, and cut so deep a gash that the blood rushed out in a stream. Some men who were not far off heard his cries and came to him, and if they had not bound his wound and carried him home, he would have died.

The next day Peter's mother said, "Peter, do you see what you have made your brothers suffer by your idleness? If you had gone into the woods as you should have done in the first place, this would not have happened. So take the axe and go now, and don't come home till you have cut that tree down." And then she gave him a hard crust of bread, and a small flask of sour milk for his lunch.

It was a long time before Peter found the tree, and when he came to it, he was both hungry and tired. He took the bread from his pocket and was just going to eat it, when the little red-faced man stood before him. "Please give me one crumb of your bread and a drop of your milk in, for I am dying of hunger and thirst," said the poor man.

"Come and sit down with me on this log," said Peter, "and I will share it all with you."

So the two sat together, side by side, and ate their lunch, and Peter thought that he had never tasted anything so good.

When they had finished, the little man said, "You are very kind-hearted, so I'll tell you a secret. When you have cut the tree down, look in the hollow stump. There you will find a strange creature that you must carry to the king. It may be that some people will try to touch the creature as you are walking along, and so you must be sure whenever it cries out, to say, 'Hold fast! Hold fast! Hold fast!'"

After the little man had gone on his way, Peter took up his axe and began to chop with all his might. The chips flew, and it was not long until the tree began to tremble, and soon it fell with a loud crash to the ground. Peter saw that there was a round hollow place in the stump, and in it sat – a goose.

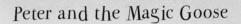

Peter thought that this was not a very strange creature after all, for he had seen geese all his life. If he had been wiser, he would have laughed at the idea of carrying it to the king, but, since the little man had told him to do so, he picked the goose up in his arms and started at once.

He made his way out of the woods, and soon came to the great road that led to the king's town. By the side of

the road there was an inn, and some men were standing in the wagonyard nearby. When Peter came up with the goose in his arms, the innkeeper's daughter, who was looking out at the door, called to him, and said, "Where did you get that pretty goose? You'll give me one of its feathers, won't you?"

"Come and pull one out," said Peter, kindly.

The girl ran out and tried to get one of the long white feathers from the bird's wing, but the moment that she touched it the goose screamed, and Peter remembered what the little man had told him to say. "Hold fast! Hold fast! Hold fast!" he cried, and the young lady's fingers stuck so fast to the goose that she could not let go. She screamed and tried her best to pull away, but Peter walked along and took no more notice of her at all.

The men who were standing in the yard laughed, for they thought that she was only making believe, but the stable boy, when he heard her cries, ran out into the road to see what was the matter.

"Oh, Tommy, Tommy help me!" cried the poor girl. "Give me your hand and set me free from this horrid goose."

"Of course I will," said Tommy, and he seized the girl's hand.

But at that very moment the goose screamed again, and Peter, without looking back, cried out, "Hold fast! Hold fast! Hold fast!"

The stable boy could not let go of the girl's hand, but was obliged to follow after her, and although he howled loudly and tried to pull away, Peter walked steadily along and seemed not to notice him.

They soon came to a village where there were a great many people out for a holiday. A circus show was about to open, and the clown was in the street doing some of his funny tricks. When he saw Peter and the girl and the stable boy passing by, he cried out, "What's the matter there? Have three more clowns come to town?"

"I am no clown," cried the stable boy, "but this girl holds my hand so tight that I can't get away. Come, set me free, and I will do you as good a turn some day."

The clown, in his droll way, seized the stable boy by the string of his apron. The goose screamed, and Peter cried out, "Hold fast! Hold fast! Hold fast!"

Of course the clown could not let go. But Peter walked on, and looked neither to the right nor to the left. When the people saw the clown trying to pull away, they thought he was only at his tricks again, and everybody laughed.

Just then the mayor of the village came walking up the street. He was a very grave, sober man who was never known to smile, and the clown's silly actions did not please him at all. "What do you mean by grinning at me?" he said, and he seized the fellow's coat tail and tried to stop him.

But at that moment the goose screamed, and Peter again cried out, "Hold fast! Hold fast! Hold fast!" What could the mayor do but follow Peter with the rest? For, try as hard as he would, he could not let go.

The wife of the mayor, a tall, spare woman, was greatly vexed when she saw her husband marching along and hanging to the clown's coat tail. She ran after him and seized his free arm and tried her best to pull him away.

The goose screamed, and Peter, without looking back, cried out, "Hold fast! Hold fast! Hold fast!"

The good lady could not help herself. She had to walk along whether she would or not, and make the best of it. A great many people followed, laughing and wondering, but none of them wanted to touch the mayor's wife – for she kept her tongue going very fast, you may be sure.

In a little while, Peter came in sight of the king's palace. Just before reaching the gates he

met a fine carriage drawn by four white horses, and in the carriage sat a young lady, as beautiful as a summer day, but with a sad and solemn look.

Peter and his train stepped aside to let the carriage pass, and just then the young lady looked out. When she saw the goose, and the funny way in which so many people had to walk behind it, she burst into a loud laugh. Then she ordered the coachman to stop, so that she might see better, and the longer she looked, the harder she laughed.

"The princess has laughed! The princess has laughed!" cried the servants that were with her, and one of them ran back to tell the king about it.

When the king heard what had happened he was delighted. He ran out to see for himself, and when he saw Peter and his train he was so amused that he laughed louder than anybody else.

"My good friend," he said to Peter, "which will you choose?"

Peter stared at him and said nothing, for he did not know what the king meant.

"Do you know what I promised to the one who would make my daughter laugh?" said the king.

"No, I don't think I do," said Peter.

"I promised a thousand dollars or a piece of land," said the king. "Which will you choose?"

"I think I'll take the land," said Peter.

Then he stroked the goose's head, and in a moment the girl and the stable boy and the clown and the mayor and the mayor's wife were suddenly free, and they were so glad to get away that they all ran home quickly as though someone had lit a fire behind them.

"What a pretty bird!" said the princess as she stepped out of her carriage and came to look at the goose. Then she reached out her pretty white hand to stroke its neck.

The goose screamed, and Peter cried out, "Hold fast! Hold fast! Hold fast!"

And the princess thought that Peter was the handsomest lad she had ever seen. The king, too, was pleased with him and gave him a fine suit of clothes, and took him into the palace to be a page and wait on the ladies at the table.

When Peter grew up to be a strong and handsome man, he became a brave knight, and he and the princess were happily married. But the starnge lgoose flew up into the air and winged its way back to the forest, and nobody has seen it from that day to this.

The End